Patrick Gloutney

Past Crush Depth

To Dale and Heather (Santa) Cockx whose yearly gift of a book every Christmas helped fuel my knowledge and my literary interests.

Crush Depth: The depth at which a submarine's hull can no long support the pressure of the surrounding water and will implode.

Prologue

It was the perfect world. Peace reigned after the collapse of human society in 2045, caused by a nuclear war, and a new attitude arose. With advanced technologies, humans were able to re-establish lost resources and rebuild planet Earth. Everyone who survived had food, water, and resources divided equally among them. However, wildlife was almost non-existent as most had died off from the radiation from the bombs. Due to a lack of DNA samples from these animals, humans couldn't regain that part of their world.

Nothing lasts forever. Soon, the old habits of humans began to surface. The women were cast down as second-class citizens, good for only cleaning, cooking and childbearing. Additionally, greed returned. Small battles began to erupt, and soon they became wars. The world became divided into the Western and Eastern hemispheres. Neither side wanted peace. All they wanted was power, and they would do anything for it. No one was foolish enough to start another nuclear war for fear of losing all they had left; at least not until December of 3679. The East began to secretly build small nuclear warheads to be shipped out on a submarine for a surprise attack on the West. When the West got word of this, they sent out their most advanced sub, the *Blue Jay,* to find the sub, disarm and retrieve the warheads to stop the attack. They lost contact with it three days after deployment...

Black Depths
of the Sea

Western Attack Submarine *Blue Jay*

"Torpedo has lost contact," the Sonar Operator called. Captain Autumn Gayle let herself breathe. The East had been waiting for them; they were no farther than 30 miles from their target when the first shot took out their communication antenna. Since then, they'd had three torpedoes on their tail. The *Blue Jay* could outrun any torpedo when it was going straight. Once it needed to turn, it was vulnerable, and the East seemed to know this. They kept cutting the *Blue Jay* off, forcing her into turns. They were able to avoid the first two torpedoes long enough for them to run out of fuel, but it was close. The third one refused to let up.

Finally, they came to an underwater mountain. Autumn ordered her crew to circle it and then bottom the vessel, hoping the torpedo would lose sonar contact in the ground clutter.

Bottoming a sub was risky. The sea floor was covered with destroyed warships and was no longer accurately mapped. The *Blue Jay* hit the floor like a hover train roaring through a station, but it worked; the torpedo lost contact.

"Damage report," Autumn demanded.

"No integrity damage. Forward tubes are blocked but not damaged. Props aren't spinning but are operational. Most of the communication equipment is down. All cameras are functional," the XO reported. Autumn looked out the windows that surrounded the bridge. Those windows were one of the *Blue Jay's* advantages. Using a special light, the crew was able to see their enemy. On top of that, all important information was projected and expertly arranged on the touch-sensitive windows.

Autumn could see three subs approaching the *Blue Jay,* surrounding the ship.

"Sonar, can they see us?"

"Not yet, but soon," Sonar Operator Sounder called.

Autumn made a quick decision.

"Prepare for emergency blow," she ordered. Her Executive Officer, or XO, Frank Lindon, gave her a disapproving look. The XO was originally the Captain of the *Blue Jay.* He was demoted rather than charged with sedition after he criticized the government while in a drunken rage. That's when Autumn took over. Ever since that day, the XO had never seemed to trust her. He wasn't the only one. There was a number of the crew that didn't like being under the command of a woman, but they followed orders and none was bold enough to voice their objection.

"Now!" Autumn ordered.

"Emergency Blow!" the XO shouted. There were a few more orders before the sub leaped off the bottom of the ocean, pushing Autumn against her seat.

"Spin up the screws," Autumn stated. Suddenly, the windows turned yellow, warning of an imminent threat.

"They have a sonar lock on us!" Sounder yelled. "Three fish in the water!" The windows turned red, indicating an immediate threat, before Autumn responded.

"All ahead flank! Surface! Surface! Surface!" One of the torpedoes' proximity detonations rocked the *Blue Jay*. Lights flashed as the frame groaned under the stress. Autumn turned and watched the remaining red outlined torpedoes continue straight. She smiled seconds before the torpedoes plowed into two of the enemy subs.

The *Blue Jay* surfaced, causing a rapid deceleration.

"Last sub's coming up!" Sonar reported. Sure enough, the enemy surfaced next to the *Blue Jay*.

"Dive! Dive! Dive!" Autumn commanded. The *Blue Jay's* bow swung low, and the frame groaned as it sank itself. The depth gauges changed so fast that they were just a blur. The windows turned yellow. The enemy was still on their tail.

"Find that mountain and head straight towards it!"

"Belay that. That will kill us!" The XO snapped.

"Do as I say!" Autumn snapped back.

"No! I refuse to take orders from an incompetent Captain," the XO reported. Autumn looked at the Helmsman, who to her relief was turning the controls.

"XO, you are relieved of duty. COB, remove him from the CON," Autumn said plainly. The XO sneered but complied and left.

The *Blue Jay* was now heading straight for the underwater mountain that had saved them before.

"One minute to impact," the computer stated.

"Sound collision alarm," Autumn said. A loud, high-pitched beep sounded three times throughout the ship. "Turn heading 230!" The Helmsman jammed the controls hard to the right, and the *Blue Jay* practically rolled onto her side as it executed the turn. Autumn hoped the ship could make it. She looked back at the sub following them. The *Blue Jay* cleared the mountain just before the enemy submarine plowed into it. The resulting explosion pitched the *Blue Jay* downward, sending it crashing onto the sea floor. It slid a good hundred meters before plowing through a wrecked destroyer, knocking Autumn from her seat. Then the *Blue Jay* hit something else, and Autumn was knocked unconscious.

Western Defence Command

The bullet flew straight and true, through the young attendant's left shoulder, and shattered a display screen mounted on the wall. The Leader of the Western hemisphere, Dale Herman, swung his weapon toward the Navy Master as the attendant fell.

"What do you mean you lost it!?" Dale asked angrily.

"The *Blue Jay* was ambushed. The external cameras were all that were talking to us. As you saw in the footage before you shot that poor man, the *Blue Jay* fought back but hit the floor shortly afterward. It's unlikely anyone survived." Dale knew that this Navy Master didn't approve of the way he shot people when he was mad. Then again, he had already shot the two previous Navy Masters in the past year. It was easy enough to avoid, though. As long as they did their jobs right, they were never in any danger.

"You told me that thing had a nearly indestructible hull, the latest in communication technologies and the ability to shoot from miles away! How is it that it was bested by three inferior Eastern vessels?" Dale demanded, desperate for a way to salvage this mission.

"We don't know, but we have a feeling that the fact a *female* was in command might have had an impact," the Navy Master growled.

This grabbed all of Dale's attention. *A female*, he thought to himself, *what kind of idiot puts a female in charge of a sub?*

"I suggest we dispatch a rescue crew, in case they did survive," one of his advisors suggested.

"I told you no one would have survived," the Navy Master snapped.

"Sir..."

"He's right. There's no use in a rescue. Any survivors will die eventually," Dale said, and then sat back to examine the footage from the *Blue Jay* exterior cameras in more detail. He was impressed by the movement of the sub. Suddenly, he realized who was in command. He stiffened in his chair.

"Who was in command of that submarine?" he asked, as he slowly rose from his seat.

The Navy Master pulled up a file on the display, "A Captain Autumn Gayle. She's had an exemplary career considering she's a woman. I doubt she was the best fit for this mission, though."

Dale nodded. He picked up a letter opener and idly twirled it between his fingers. The Navy Master was right. Autumn was not the best fit for the mission, only not for the reasons he believed. Dale approached the Navy Master slowly, "Who decided to send her?"

"You wanted our best," the Navy Master replied, unfazed by Dale's approach. "You made Captain Gayle Commander of the *Blue Jay* some time ago. She may not have been the best, but her ship was."

Dale grabbed the man's head, "You do not send a lamb into slaughter," he growled, running the letter opener over the man's throat and then lifting his chin with it.

"The *Blue Jay* was our best chance to defeat the Eastern submarine battle group. You approved its deployment," the Navy Master defended.

Dale smiled, "I did, didn't I?" With that, Dale quickly drives his letter opener through the Navy Master's hand. The man howled in pain.

"I didn't, however, approve the crew. When the *Blue Jay* returns, make her crew available," Dale ordered. The Navy Master nodded vigorously, wrapping his hand in his jacket.

"You are dismissed." No one wasted any time leaving.

"Navy Master," Dale called.

"Y...Yes, Sir," the Navy Master responded shakily.

"Get that looked at before it becomes infected, and for God's sake, stop bleeding on my floor."

"Right away, sir."

Western Attack Submarine *Blue Jay*

Autumn forced herself to sit up. Her head was throbbing, and the flashing yellow lights didn't help. She slowly made it to her feet and walked across the bridge. There were bodies everywhere, but the number was fewer than the bridge crew, so some must still be alive. As she reached the helm, she noticed a flashing blue light. She had no idea why this light interested her. There were hundreds of lights flashing, but only one blue light. When she realized what it meant, her heart sank. It signified a radiation leak. She grabbed the intercom.

"This is the Captain." Her voice was shaking. She took a moment to steady herself, then continued, "Stations report," was all she could manage.

"Ma'am," someone said softly off to her left. Autumn moved towards the voice and found the Sonar Operator, Sounder, with his hand stretched out towards her. She grabbed the hand, happy for any human contact. She knew Sounder from her time as a helm operator. He had a bad cut to the head and was pinned under a fallen panel.

"Tell my wife I—" Autumn did her best to hold back her tears.

"You tell her yourself. We're going to make it back, understand." She was harsher than she wanted. Sounder smiled and placed his hand on her cheek.

"You always had such spirit. Can you still help Maya with her school project?" Sounder's voice was growing weak. Autumn nodded her head. Mya, Sounder's daughter, was doing a project in school about the Western defences, more specifically, women in the system. Sounder had asked that Autumn provide some insight. Autumn gripped Sounder's hand tightly as he began to cough up blood. He smiled at her, took a deep breath and then his body went limp. Autumn finally let a tear fall. She pulled herself together when she heard people coming up the ladder.

"Captain!" the COB called. He was accompanied by the XO. Autumn didn't respond. She was still holding Sounder's hand.

"Doesn't look like she made it," the XO said a bit too happily.

"I wouldn't be so quick to jump to a conclusion," Autumn said, releasing Sounder's hand.

"Bless the Lord, you're alive," the COB said.

"What happened to the rest of the crew?" Autumn asked. COB and the XO exchanged a look. "Well, let's hear it!"

"Everyone who was able met in the gallery after the impact. We determined that there was water in the forward cargo hold, but it was sealed, and that some of the water-tight doors closed, trapping people in certain sections. It's hard to say which, as many sections aren't responding," the COB explained.

"Cut to the chase, COB. What happened to the crew, and how many are left?" Autumn was getting frustrated. She could tell that the COB was beating around the bush.

"There is a cooling line for the reactor that runs through the galley. It cracked for some reason. The XO and I managed to divert the line before it affected the reactor, but when we got back..."

"They were all dead," the XO stated plainly.

Autumn collapsed into her chair. *That explained the radiation alarm.*

"Can we fight?" Autumn asked. The COB and XO looked at her, bewildered. She gave them a look that said, "*Well?*"

"The Sonar Operator, Jones, made it, and there is a Weapons Operator awaiting orders. We may have men in the torpedo room, but I have no idea what shape the engine room is in," The COB stated.

Autumn remembered her previous call to the crew. She grabbed the intercom. "Anyone who can, you are ordered to report to the bridge."

A few minutes of silence followed. Autumn was about to give up when a call came through. "Torpedo room."

Thank God, Autumn thought to herself. "Damage report." Just then, the second intercom beeped, and the XO grabbed it.

"No structural damage, but there are only three of us alive down here. The door closed before we could get out," the man in the torpedo room reported.

"Can we fire torpedoes?" Autumn asked.

"I think so. The three of us can load and repair anything that's broken," the man reported. Autumn let herself relax a little. They could fight if the engine was working.

"Thanks. Sit tight. We'll try and get those doors open," she said and cut the call.

She looked to the XO, who was finishing his call. "The engine is functional. There is a minor problem with one of the transformers, but they can fix it. There are five alive down there." The two of them waited until the COB came back with a Weapons Operator, the Sonar Operator Jones, and a Communication Officer.

"That's all we got. The rest are dead," the COB said, his voice sounding distant.

"How the hell are we going to move without a Helmsman?" the XO asked the COB angrily.

"I'll drive," Autumn said. Everyone on the bridge stared at her. "I used to be the Helmsman. XO, you will have to call commands, but I'm still in charge. If I say shoot you find something to shoot. Understand?" The XO nodded. "Good. Someone shut off these lights."

Soon, the lighting was back to normal, and Autumn was carefully lifting the *Blue Jay* off the sea floor. She spun up the screws, and the speed indicator clicked upwards. Autumn was relieved to find that none of the controls were damaged.

"Put some fish in those tubes," Autumn said.

Eastern Nuclear Launch Submarine *Titan*

"Sir, report on the subs that went after the *Blue Jay*." The Petty Officer handed Trent a clipboard. Trent sighed as he read the paper. Three subs, destroyed, not one torpedo from *Blue Jay was* reported fired. The report also detailed that despite its size, the *Blue Jay* was very agile. This one fact alone posed a huge threat to the *Titan*. Weighed down with the nukes and running on older diesel engines, *Titan* could do five knots tops underwater and seven on the surface. She was so slow, it took her three minutes to alter course by ten degrees. Trent glanced at the list of escorts he had with him. All ran on diesel engines, and although they were faster than *Titan,* they still couldn't outmaneuver the *Blue Jay.* Trent shook his head and grabbed the intercom.

"CON to Engineering. We need to increase our speed, now."

"We're already running at max RPM; we can't give you any more," the engineer reported back.

"Can we do anything to make *Titan* less of a slug?" Trent asked.

"Negative. We'd have to drop some nukes."

"Roger that. CON out." Trent pounded his fist against a support beam.

"I want every sub to surface," Trent ordered. His XO gave him a look.

"Sir, that will expose us. We should use the snorkels." Large steel poles that extended from the back of a diesel sub, the snorkels allowed the powerful diesel engines to run and charge the battery while the sub was still underwater, making it less visible from the air. However, because of the shape of the *Titan's* hull, it could still only do 5 knots when using a snorkel.

"Surface vessel, keep one under for sonar sweeps. All subs should maintain at least 80% battery power and be on constant lookout for aircraft. We need to gain speed," Trent ordered.

Western Airborne Gunship *Shredder,*

James was still trying to wrap his head around his orders. He was instructed to locate the *Blue Jay,* try to raise her on the radio, and if they got no response, they were to destroy the wreckage. How could the Navy's most advanced submarine just die? They were almost on top of its last known position when he gave up pondering the question.

"Anything on the radar?" James asked. The *Shredder* was a large airborne gunship shaped like the F-16s used before the Nuclear War. It was manned by about 150 men and was only needed when there was a lot to blow up. It was, as its name suggests, a killing machine. With its high-power small-calibre cannons mounted on the nose, it was able to snipe a man from 35,000 feet with up to one-inch accuracy on a stormy day.

"Yes, sir, one contact at four miles, it's the *Blue Jay:* she's deep," the Radar Operator reported. The *Shredder's* radar was powerful enough to locate vessels underwater, but only in a five-mile radius.

"No response on the radio," the First Officer said. James sighed. He was against the idea, but orders were orders.

"Lock it. Let's make this quick," he ordered.

"Movement! Her screws are spinning! Bearing 345 degrees, speed 12 knots," the Radar Operator called.

"Helm, maintain silence. Fly the Pattern," James said, "See if you recognize theirs." The *Shredder* instantly fell into a 90° bank and made a tight circle over where the *Blue Jay* was. Then it shot into a short climb before descending to 100 feet and flying parallel with the *Blue Jay's* course. Then James thought of something.

"Let's make sure they know it's us. Helm, dip the wing," he ordered. The *Shredder's* frame was extremely strong and could take multiple blows from a missile. They had in the past, during airshows, done this manoeuver, so it would be like signing a letter with DNA. James loved watching, so he looked out the window just as the left wingtip sliced into the water. It didn't even upset the *Shredder.* The helm pulled a wide circle, keeping the wingtip underwater, then reared up on it and rolled up away from the water, wrapping a huge wave of water around them. Once it reached 1000 feet, they began to slow and circle the *Blue Jay* again. James hoped the sub wasn't too damaged to surface. Then, as if to answer his question, the *Blue Jay* surfaced off to the right, its blue markings glowing brightly. Its anti-aircraft cannons spun upwards and fired a blank shot to show it complied with the pattern. James wasn't sure, but he thought that the ship looked battered.

"Sir," the First Officer said, handing James a headset.

James put it on, "Airborne Gunship *Shredder* to Attack Submarine *Blue Jay,* come in."

"*Blue Jay* to *Shredder,* this is the Captain speaking. Are we ever glad to see you," a voice said over the short-wave radio. James felt himself gag. He had half a mind to blow the *Blue Jay* sky high right then and there. The one thing he knew should never be allowed to happen was talking to him on the radio. The Captain of the most advanced ship in the Western Navy was unmistakably a *woman.*

Western Attack Submarine *Blue Jay,*

"*Shredder,* come in, do you read?" Autumn radioed. She looked at the Communications Officer, who began to turn some dials.

"The shortwave radio is working. They are getting the transmission," he reported back. Autumn sighed. She knew what had happened; it had happened many times before. The guy on the other end heard she was a woman and was going to leave her to die.

"What's wrong, Ma'am? They ignoring a woman?" the XO chuckled. Autumn ignored him.

"*Blue Jay* to *Shredder* come in!" Suddenly, Autumn felt dizzy. It was like the *Blue Jay* had begun to spin downwards. She grabbed a pipe for balance.

"You alright, Ma'am?" The COB asked.

"We need to get to a port," Autumn stated plainly. She was sure she had a concussion, and there was no telling what shape the crews in the engine room and weapons bay were in. "I want one blank in the cannons, and the rest are live. Aim at the *Shredder* and lock them when I say."

"Ma'am, you can't possibly..."

"Best way to get their attention, that's why the first shot's a blank," Autumn said sternly. "*Blue Jay* to *Shredder* come in, damn it. Or face the consequences of violating an order." Autumn hoped she had guessed right. She assumed that their orders were to locate and retrieve the *Blue Jay*. When no response came, she sighed again. "Lock it."

"Target locked, it's rolling...climbing...trying to turn away," the Weapons Operator called.

"Fire," Autumn ordered. She felt the ship lurch sideways from the recoil of the massive cannons positioned on her back.

"*Blue Jay* to *Shredder* come in or the next one does damage."

"Who the hell do you think you are?" the *Shredder's* Captain radioed, obviously enraged.

"I suggest you grow up. I would hate to put a hole in the *Shredder*," Autumn said sternly. "What are your orders?" Autumn could hear displeasure on the other end of the line.

"We were ordered to find you, contact you, and if the worst had happened, destroy you," the Captain said.

"Can you relay our radio transmission?" Autumn asked.

"Why not use your SATCOM?"

"It was destroyed," Autumn stated, then a wave of nausea hit her.

"Did the little girl lead her big ship into a trap?" the *Shredder's* Captain mocked. Autumn suppressed her urge to vomit and turned to the Weapons Operator.

"They don't need the probe on the nose right now," she said plainly. The Weapons Operator took the hint, and soon the ship lurched as the cannons fired again. Autumn looked out the window in time to see an explosion erupt on the *Shredder's* nose. That would get her point across.

"I swear the next goes into your engine," she snapped.

"We'll relay the transmission," came the reply. And soon the radio crackled to life with a new voice.

"Hello?" Autumn cringed. The *Shredder* had linked her in with Dale Herman. She swallowed the lump in her throat and replied.

"Captain Autumn Gayle of the *Blue Jay* reporting, sir."

"Autumn! I'm so glad you're alive," Dale's joyful voice gave the illusion that there was something special between him and Autumn. Granted, Autumn had taken advantage of his infatuation to get her where she was. "Are you–I mean, what is the condition of your ship?"

"We were ambushed. Our communication system was destroyed. We destroyed three ships but hit the floor after an evasive manoeuver. A radiation leak killed most of the crew," Autumn reported.

"Radiation leak! Oh dear, are you safe in that sub?" Dale asked.

"Perfectly,"

"Can you fight?" Dale inquired.

"We can, but the crew is reduced to a few on the CON, a couple in with the engines and some in the torpedo room," Autumn stated.

"Very good. You are to continue your mission as planned." Autumn felt a stab of betrayal. He didn't care for her as much as she had thought. She was just another officer in his Navy.

"Sir, I said we can fight. We are in no way battle-ready," Autumn argued quickly.

"It is imperative that this mission is successful. I wouldn't be asking you if I had another option," Dale responded, his tone hardening.

"Send the *Shredder.*"

"It would do nothing. They would dive, and the *Shredder* would be able to do nothing," Dale stated plainly. Autumn knew what he meant. Although the *Shredder* was equipped with torpedoes, it couldn't dive as deep as the enemy. The *Blue Jay,* however, could.

"Think of your mother." Dale's voice had softened to a gentle, caring sound. Autumn winced at the thought of her mother. The poor woman had been involved in a hovercraft accident and was now in the hospital, paralyzed from the waist down. Dale was the head of the government, and the government controlled all healthcare. Dales was threatening to pull the plug on her mother! Autumn sighed and saw no point in arguing.

"Very well, sir. We will turn back on course immediately," Autumn cut the radio.

"Ma'am, you can't possibly be thinking we can succeed," the XO asked from behind her.

"We will succeed. For all those back home. If we can't stop them, there won't be time to deploy another sub," Autumn said.

"Like he said, an air raid on the sub would be useless," the COB piped up.

"*Shredder* to *Blue Jay*, disarm your guns." The voice was steady, but Autumn could detect the fear behind it. This was not the Captain. It must have been the First Officer.

Autumn nodded to the Weapons Operator.

"Thank you. I hope you like us because we have been ordered to help in any way possible."

This intrigued Autumn. The use of the *Shredder* might just give them a chance. "How good a shot are you guys?"

Eastern Escort Sub #6

"Sub Seven has surfaced and Sub Nine is diving to take its post," a voice called from across the CON. Captain Demetri nodded. Their setup had worked so far. Although he would have preferred to stay submerged, the *Titan* was adamant that they needed to stay above the water. This was their most vulnerable time. With one sub surfacing and the other diving, they would have limited sonar coverage, and that could give the *Blue Jay* a window of opportunity.

"New inbound! Low 500 feet...big...fast...it's a gunship!" a Radar Operator shouted.

"Alert all subs! Make sure *Titan* gets her fat ass down before it gets here," Demetri ordered. He longed to be on the *Titan* despite her sluggishness. In the East, it was no big deal to command a sub, but to command one with a name, not a number, that was a great honour normally reserved for submarine aces or heroes. His sub had no defence against aircraft, and if they were hit, they would bear the wound for the rest of the trip, and the enemy would fly away unharmed.

"Inbound 30 seconds out," the radar operator called.

"*Titan* is under," the XO reported.

"Dive! Dive! Dive!" Demetri ordered. Sub Six's bow swung down quickly and was soon 50 feet under. It slowed its dive and speed to match that of the *Titan*. Then an explosion rocked the ship, its frame groaned, and the whole ship rolled into a turn.

"Torpedo destroyed Sub Five," someone reported.

"Helm, level us out!" Demetri ordered.

"No response from the controls." Then the ship came to a sudden stop. The deceleration knocked Demetri off his feet; the frame let out a mighty groan, and the ship drifted backward.

"Report!"

"We hit Sub Seven broadside. She's going down."

"Taking on water in all forward compartments. Gaining depth."

"New sub contact! Bearing one-five-zero degrees!"

"Fire at them!" Demetri ordered. Seconds later, he heard a torpedo leave one of the undamaged tubes. He was grateful none of their torpedoes had exploded in the collision. "Emergency blow!" Demetri saw the Ballast Operator yank on a lever, but nothing happened.

"No response from the controls!" someone shouted.

"Restart the System!" Demetri called, but it was too late. Sub Six hit the sea floor at a forty-five-degree angle, her damaged bow taking the worst of it. The sub's frame screeched in protest as she rolled onto her side. Images of his childhood, of his wife and son, flashed before Demetri's eyes. He was brought back to reality when a fuel line burst to fill the CON with diesel fumes. Then everything fell quiet; the only sounds were people coughing on the fumes and the metal frame of the sub groaning. Demetri looked at the depth gauges; its needle was well below the marked scale. Sub Six was never meant to go so deep. Then the wall in front of Demetri gave one last groan and buckled inward. It tore the electrical system, sending a shower of sparks down at Demetri. Water rushed in. They would have all surely drowned if sparks from the severed electrical system had not ignited the diesel fumes filling the CON. The crew died in a ball of flames before the water filled the bridge.

Past Crush Depth

Western Airborne Gunship *Shredder,*

Even James had to admit that it was an impressive plan. The *Blue Jay* had fired one torpedo, which blew the first enemy sub out of the water. Because of the tight formation in which the subs were travelling, the shock wave from the explosion damaged the second and third subs. The third sub was sent spinning away from the formation while the fourth got stuck in a turn and plowed into a fifth sub. The last two subs both began to fall. The third sub regained control and circled back to the formation, but was shot by its escort, mistaking it for the *Blue Jay.* Amid all the confusion and panic, the *Blue Jay* had slipped into a vacant spot in the enemy's formation. James was still kicking himself for being outsmarted by a woman. The stunt with her guns was bad enough, and now the plan he said would never work had gone off without a hitch.

"Alright, it's our turn to show off. Bring her around," James ordered. The *Shredder* rolled onto her starboard wing and pulled a tight turn.

"Call 'em as soon as we lock 'em," James said. They were no more than a hundred feet off the water now. Thankfully, the target sub didn't have any anti-aircraft capabilities.

"Locked one of the two remaining subs," Weapons called.

"Fire." Two torpedoes dropped from the wings of the *Shredder,* splashing into the water, powering towards their targets. *Shredder* was just finishing its turn for another pass when one explosion erupted. The time between launch and detonation was too short for James. *Why isn't Titan going deeper?*

"Torpedo one hit target. Second Torpedo won't lock!"

"What? Why?" James demanded.

"Malfunction in sonar. Rebooting the system now," someone reported. James slammed his fist onto his armrest in frustration. *We were supposed to be showing them up,* he thought. Yet again, that woman and her ship had bested him and the *Shredder.*

"Four new contacts! Bearing one-four-six degrees, high...small...they're Eastern fighters!" Radar reported.

"Damn it," James grumbled.

"Fighter contacts changing to intercept course. ETA four minutes!"

"Sonar rebooted."

"Helm, line us up!" James ordered. The *Shredder* readjusted its course.

"Sir! Subs are nearing the limits of our weapons. We can no longer guarantee a solid lock-on," the First Officer stated.

"We fire. We can't let that joke of a Captain think we can't follow through," James said, his voice cold as ice.

"Sir, I think this has become more about beating the *Blue Jay* than destroying the *Titan,*" the First Officer responded, his tone equally cold. James ignored him.

"Faint lock on target two."

"Fire!"

"Enemy fighter closing; ETA one minute."

"Full power, climb and evade," James ordered.

"Torpedo one on course...tracking...target destroyed," someone yelled.

"Fighter chasing!" Radar reported.

"Max afterburner. Leave it in the dust."

"Torpedo two lost contact. Searching for new contact."

"Sir, we must destroy it!" the First Officer demanded.

"No, keep her going," James said firmly. Bullets from one of the Eastern fighters raked across the *Shredder's* back. In response, the Helmsman yanked the *Shredder* into a steep climb, then dove on the assailant. They rolled inverted and fired on the enemy fighter with the cannons mounted on their back. James would have preferred to use the nose cannons, but the *Blue Jay* had made that impossible.

"Torpedo two found new target..."

"What's it tracking?" James barked.

"The *Blue Jay.*" James' heartbeats hammered in his ears as the bridge fell silent.

"Destroy it," James said softly. He glanced at the altimeter next to his seat. They had gained considerable height in the fight with the fighter, and he wasn't sure they would be able to contact the torpedo. Someone heard his weak order because they confirmed his suspicions.

"Unable to contact torpedo two."

Western Attack Submarine *Blue Jay*

The glass turned red, and Autumn instinctively jammed the throttles to **MAX** and pushed the *Blue Jay* into a dive. *What had gone wrong?* she asked herself. *How did they figure out who we are?* Then she got her answer when the Sonar Operator reported.

"One of *Shredder's* torpedoes locked us!"

Autumn rolled her eyes. *And women are inferior?* She put the *Blue Jay* into a turn in an attempt to confuse the torpedo.

"Fifteen seconds to detonation," the computer reported. The outline of a sub appeared on the display. Autumn was about to turn away from it when she got an idea.

"Hold on!" She called and, without waiting for a response, she pushed the bow down. Once they were right under the other sub, she threw the blast Controls to **BLOW**, and the *Blue Jay* began a steep ascent.

"Detonation in five, four, three, two, one..." Autumn had managed to put the other submarine between the *Blue Jay* and the torpedo. The torpedo hit the enemy sub, destroying it. The shock wave slammed into the *Blue Jay's* flank, pushing her into a spinning dive. Autumn hit her head on the controls. She tried her best to level the *Blue Jay's* dive, but her vision was beginning to blur. Her hand groped along the controls but could not distinguish one control from another. She hopelessly pulled on the controls, but they were locked in place.

"Flooding in cargo bay two, closing watertight doors," the computer called, although Autumn barely heard it over the alarms.

"Restart the Control System," Autumn ordered, her voice beginning to slur. If she hadn't had a concussion before, she had one now. She wasn't sure if she had spoken loud enough, but someone must have heard because the controls snapped free and the bow swung upwards. Autumn levelled the dive and pulled alongside the *Titan*. She programmed the computer to continue in its formation position and then slumped back in her chair, her head throbbing. She had only just heard the radio call from *Titan*.

"All escorts, this is *Titan*. Report." Autumn knew everyone was looking at her. She fought through the confusion she was facing and managed to speak if you could call it speaking. It sounded like she had just downed five bottles of pure alcohol.

"XO answer. They...won't believe...if...I answer." The XO nodded, and the COB approached Autumn's side.

"You all right, Ma'am? That was some impressive sailing," he said, clearly concerned.

"I'm...fine. I just need to stand," was all Autumn could muster. She could see the XO watching her, no doubt thinking of a way to overthrow her and take control. She stood up, grasping at a handrail for support.

"Did you take a hit to the head, Ma'am? I think you..." Autumn never heard the end of the sentence. She fell to her knees and passed out.

Her mind was a blur of images and sound; it hurt to move, it hurt to think. She could see the Blue Jay *slamming into the sea floor, her crew dying. She could see her family, happy as can be, at a picnic at the park by her old house. Then the images cleared, and she was left sitting in a hospital room beside her mother's bed. She could see a man standing in the doorway. His clothes were black, and he didn't seem to have a face. The man moved towards her mother. He did something to the machine, keeping her alive, and then he left. At first, Autumn couldn't figure out what was going on, and then she noticed that the man had changed the IV drip. The liquid was not clear anymore; it was murky green. Autumn tried to call as her mother's heartbeat slowed, but no words came out. It felt like her mouth was filled with cement. She tried to move, but her limbs were rigid. An alarm went off warning the nurse of her mother's problem, but no one came. All Autumn could do was sit and watch in horror as her mother died.*

A hand slapped across her face.

"Autumn. Wake up, goddamn it!" the COB shouted, shaking Autumn out of her daze. She couldn't remember if the COB had ever called her by her first name before. She sat up, her head throbbing.

"What happened?" she asked.

"You took a hit to the head. We need to get you home," the COB said.

"No, we can't go back yet. We need those warheads," Autumn responded, feeling her strength coming back.

"Ma'am, you can't possibly think–" the COB began, but Autumn interrupted him.

"Do you have someone you love, COB?" The COB seemed to hesitate, but Autumn didn't give it much thought as she made her way to the helm.

"Yes, Ma'am."

"If we turn back now, you'll lose them all," Autumn stated glumly.

"She's right, COB. She would know, being the Leader's squeeze and all," the XO said harshly. Autumn shot him a look.

The CON fell silent before Autumn spoke. "Anyone got any ideas?"

"Do we have to take the warheads from *Titan*? Could we just shoot her?" the Sonar Operator asked.

"Our orders are to get the warheads. Besides, if we blow her and hit a warhead, we're all dead."

"If we're going to take *Titan* with so few crews, then we'll need her on the surface," the XO observed.

"How do we do that?" the COB asked. "The second they see us, they'll dive. She's slow but not that slow." They continued the discussion. Autumn sat back. Her head still hurt, but was getting better. She listened for a way to capture the sub they were now shadowing. She was about to give up when a thought came to her.

"XO," she said, interrupting the argument the XO was having with the Weapons Operator. The XO turned to face Autumn but said nothing. "You served on diesel subs before. What would make them surface, and stay surfaced?" The XO thought for a moment, then responded.

"Carbon monoxide." Autumn saw the COB's eyes light up, but she couldn't figure out what the XO meant.

"I'm a little slow on the pickup right now."

"On a diesel sub, there's an exhaust ventilation system. If there's a big enough hole in the ducts, then the exhaust enters the main body and the scrubbers can't keep up. There's an alarm to let the crew know if the gas reaches dangerous levels," the XO explained, clearly happy to show up the Captain with his knowledge of *Titan* operations.

"And the protocol is to surface?"

"No. Protocol is to reach periscope depth and vent. But if the vents don't work, say damaged by a near miss from a torpedo, they would need to surface and evacuate, fix the hole and manually open the vents."

"How do we create an exhaust leak from here?" Autumn asked, finally able to follow the conversation. There was no response from the XO.

"We may not have to." The COB said. "Do we know how much of *Titan* is computer-controlled?"

"Most of her systems, including the alarms and vents," the Communication Officer said, reading off a display.

"Are you suggesting we hack *Titan*?" Autumn asked, stunned. Surely *Titan's* computers were protected by the latest firewalls and other security devices as were the *Blue Jay's*? "Can it be done?"

"It will take time, but I could do it," Jones said. Everyone looked at him. "I wasn't always a Sonar Operator. I used to hack for the government's spy division. For years, we accessed the East's Naval Control System. That system feeds into each sub, and when I was transferred to Naval Operations, we were starting to cause problems within their fleet."

Autumn frowned. It was typical of the government. This man would have done great work for his world, and now he was a lowly Petty Officer because of some pathetic excuse for his transfer-the definition of wasting good men.

"Alright, let's get to it," Autumn ordered. Two hours later, they were in.

Eastern Nuclear Launch Submarine *Titan*

"This is not a final damage report, sir. It contains only the loss of escorts and a few damages we sustained. The maintenance crews are still checking everything out," the *Titan's* XO told Trent. Trent grabbed the papers and reviewed them. They had lost every escort except Sub Eight. Luckily, the *Blue Jay* had been foolish enough to head straight for them, making an easy target for the *Titan's* torpedoes. Even with the destruction of their enemy, Trent couldn't shake the feeling that something bad was going to happen.

"Let me know when the final report is ready," he told the XO. Suddenly, a loud, gravelly alarm sounded and yellow lights began to flash. A display to the left of Trent turned red, and a diagram of the *Titan* appeared, displaying all of the compartments where the CO alarms were going off. It was widespread.

Trent wasted no time giving his order, "Periscope depth and open vents." Thankfully, they were already close to the surface. A carbon monoxide leak this widespread could render the *Titan* a ghost ship very quickly.

"Vents not responding. Must have been damaged in the fight."

"Carbon monoxide level's nearing critical levels, sir," the XO reported. Trent sighed. He didn't want to surface, but he had no choice.

"Surface and evacuate to the upper deck," he ordered. The evacuation, although necessary for the safety of the crew, would put the *Titan* in a very dangerous position. On the surface, with no one below deck, they would have little chance should an armed aircraft fly by. The gravelly alarm changed to a monotone sound that played in groups of three in three-second intervals. The CON soon cleared, and the XO fell into step with Trent.

"I want maintenance crews with respirators to fix the problem, and I want those vents open. We need to be underway as soon as possible." Because the danger came from their engines, *Titan* had to shut them down if they were to have any hope of clearing the deadly gas from the interior. This left *Titan* a sitting duck, with no way to maneuver and no surface-to-air defences. She wouldn't stand a chance against even a fishing vessel.

Trent climbed down from the *Titan's* tower and did a quick survey of the scene. It was pouring rain, and the swells were rocking the *Titan* back and forth slightly. The *Titan* was not what you would call streamlined. She was boxy, with a cylindrical tower extending from her midsection, surrounded by a maze of box-like silos that stored the tips of her missiles. At her bow was a large dome which contained radar and sonar equipment. Trent had never seen her belly, as she had never been dry docked during his time as Captain. But frankly, he wasn't sure he wanted to see it right now.

He was almost finished assessing the situation when something at the *Titan's* stern grabbed his attention. The water off their starboard side had a bright blue tint to it. He was puzzled at first until he remembered the photos of the *Blue Jay* sitting in port, her bright *blue* markings glowing in the dim light. He watched in horror as the *Blue Jay* surfaced before him. Trent had to turn away from the blinding light. Once the light subsided, he looked back at the sub.

Despite his resentment of it, even Trent had to admit she was impressive. It was evident it hadn't escaped the action without damage and that made him smile. Not all her markings were lit. Some were just flickering, and her flank was scarred. Crumpled metal extended from below the water line up to her midsection. As Trent looked to her stern, he saw that the rudder extending above the water line was mangled and probably useless.

Movement on the *Blue Jay's* back caught Trent's eye. He looked to see her cannon pointing towards the *Titan's* stern. He saw the flash before hearing the sound. The *Titan's* stern was forced away from the *Blue Jay*. The movement was so violent that it knocked Trent off the side of the vessel and if not for the restraints everyone had to wear on the upper deck, he would have drifted away.

"Sir!" The XO called and rushed to help him back onto the *Titan's* back. Once he had his footing, Trent looked back towards the *Titan's* stern. It looked mainly undamaged, at least what was above the water line.

Why shoot the stern? Trent asked himself. The most effective way to sink the *Titan* would be to have shot her midsection where the nukes were stored. But then the *Blue Jay* would most likely have been destroyed as well. Even so, they would have benefited more from shooting a hole in her at the water line. Then a sickening thought came to Trent. They weren't trying to sink the *Titan*. They were trying to *maim* her.

As if to confirm his worries, a panel on the *Blue Jay's* side opened, and a small black watercraft came speeding out. Trent's crew began to fire. The *Blue Jay* nearly rolled onto her side as she fired once again. This time, it took out the dome on the *Titan's* bow.

That's one powerful gun, Trent thought to himself and then hollered, "Cease fire!" The gunfire subsided, and the black watercraft beached itself on the *Titan's* hull. Three people climbed out. There were two well-built men and one woman. The men seemed sound, but the woman looked like she was fighting to stand straight. Trent drew his pistol as they approached.

"What is the meaning of this attack?" he asked.

"You are to surrender the *Titan* to us immediately by order of the Western government," the woman stated firmly. Trent laughed.

"We are, are we? You don't look much like a sailor," Trent mocked and turned to his crew. "We've seen better in the gutters back home!" Trent pointed his pistol at the man immediately to the left of the woman.

"Now let your Captain speak. What is the meaning of this attack?"

"The Captain was speaking," the man stated. The sound of the man's voice surprised Trent. He knew it from somewhere. Then he remembered. It was the voice of the man reporting on Sub Eight. The *Blue Jay* had been with them since the attack! Trent turned his gun back to the woman.

"So, the West is putting *females* in charge of ships now, are they?" The woman inclined her head. Trent frowned. "Then they are weak." He cocked the hammer on his gun. Suddenly, a tremendous bang sounded from the *Blue Jay's* cannon, and the *Titan* jolted sideways. Trent held his footing, but the *Blue Jay* boarding party disappeared into the maze of missile silos.

"Those..." Trent let his sentence trail off as a loud screeching filled the air. He looked behind him to see the *Titan's* tower falling. It crashed into the ship's side, opening a gash that would sink her if not attended to. The crew rushed below deck, the carbon monoxide threat ignored. Right now, their priority was to keep the *Titan* afloat.

A shot rang out, and one of *Titan's* crew fell into the sea. Trent whirled around and caught a glimpse of a silver pistol disappearing behind a missile block. He made his way toward it and jumped someone, but unfortunately, it was one of his crew. More shots rang out from the few guns on board. Shooting at anything that moved. The fact that they might hit another crew member was ignored.

Trent caught glimpses of moving figures, but nothing he could shoot at. He ran after the next movement he saw. He exited the missile silos to find twenty of his crew surrounding the boarding party. He smiled and approached the Westerners. All in all, they were vastly outnumbered with more crew approaching from the bow.

"You now see that the East is far superior to yourselves," Trent sneered, raising his weapon. One of the men from the *Blue Jay* stepped in front of the others. Trent didn't hesitate. He fired. The shot tore through the man's shoulder. The man fell to the ground, clearly in pain. Trent motioned with his gun for the others to back away, and they did. He walked up to the man and aimed at his head.

"Very clever; a worthy sacrifice. I'm glad, though, that I get to personally kill the *Blue Jay's* Captain."

"Very well, claim your prize," the man spat. Then someone knocked Trent off his feet. He lost his grip on his pistol and watched helplessly as the sea claimed it. He grabbed hold of an antenna on the *Titan's* back as another wave crashed over the deck. He pulled himself to his feet, and a fist met his face. He had been knocked down by the woman. He looked to his crew, knowing they wouldn't engage. This was his ship, and this was his fight to defend it.

He looked back at the woman who had knocked him down, "Who are you?"

"I am the Captain of the *Blue Jay,* and you are a threat to its survival," the woman responded.

"I have to admire your dedication to your crew," Trent lunged for her and barely managed to knock her down.

"She's lying. I'm the Captain of the *Blue Jay,*" the man Trent had shot hollered. He couldn't figure this out. It was clear one was lying, but which one? Surely the West wasn't stupid enough to put a female in charge of a sub, but there was something about the woman that made him believe she was the rightful Captain.

Trent tried to hold down the woman, but she managed to get to her feet. Her hand-to-hand combat skills were crude at best but effective. Trent noticed that she was not in the best of shape. He eventually pinned her to a missile silo.

"You know, there is one advantage to having a woman onboard," he said, looking down at her slightly unbuttoned shirt. Trent watched her squirm and laughed.

"Once I kill your Captain, you will become my little toy. You live in exchange for certain pleasures?" Trent proposed, pulling her body closer to his.

"Don't kid yourself, I would rather die."

"You can't win. I am superior. Take my courtesy. It is best for you."

"You call this courtesy?" she asked. Trent nodded. "Go to hell."

Before Trent could respond, he felt the cold metal of a blade pierce his skin. He felt it slide into the left side of his chest. He staggered backward, sliding off the knife. The pain was overwhelming as it bloomed across his body. Blood filled his lungs, cutting off his breathing. He clutched his wound and continued to back up. He couldn't believe it. A woman had bested him, had stabbed him. He wanted to take her and blow her head off, but he had lost his gun. He didn't even notice the edge of the *Titan's* deck approaching. A wave swept over the *Titan's* stern, taking him with it. He didn't fight. He let the water fill his lungs, and he died alongside his ship.

Eastern Nuclear Launch Submarine *Titan*

Shaking, Autumn managed to pull herself away from the missile silo. She rested her hand on her hip and realized that she still had her gun; she was sure she had lost it earlier. She sheathed her blood-coated knife and drew the pistol. She and the COB quickly helped the XO, and then she turned to the *Titan's* XO.

"Get your men to disarm all your missiles and place the warheads in our boat," she demanded.

"I don't take orders from a woman."

"Do it or I shoot," Autumn said, trying to steady her shaking arm as she aimed.

"You won't shoot. You're weak," the *Titan's* XO replied.

Autumn swung her weapon off to her left and fired. Another of the *Titan's* crew fell into the sea. She was sure they would return fire, but they didn't.

"Next one goes into you," Autumn snapped angrily.

"You won't shoot me. You need–" Autumn pulled the trigger before he could finish. The bullet wrenched the man's leg out from underneath him. He cried out in pain. Autumn approached, finding it easier to control her swimming head. The man looked up at her and then at her pistol. His eyes filled with fear.

"I swear to you that the next one is in your head if you don't do as I say," Autumn growled.

"Chief! See to it!" the man ordered frantically.

Autumn smiled and turned back to the COB.

"How's the XO?" she asked, kneeling beside them.

"He'll live, but he needs a hospital," the COB responded.

"We all need a hospital," Autumn said, massaging her temples. "How are you feeling, XO?"

"My shoulders are on fire, but other than that, I'm fine," the XO responded. "Thank you, by the way. I'd be dead right now if not for you." Autumn knew how hard it was for the XO to be gracious to her.

"Well, I have to thank you as well. You could have easily stuck with the truth. Instead, you allowed me to attack." Autumn smiled. "Why didn't you rat me out?" she asked softly.

"Because the *Blue Jay* needs her Captain. We all need our Captain," the XO responded.

Autumn stood up, shocked at what the XO had just said. It was the first time he had said anything of the sort to her. He always treated her as an annoyance and a crippling feature to the *Blue Jay*. Her smile broadened, and she helped him to his feet.

"We need our XO too," she said. The XO laughed.

"I nearly killed us all during the ambush," he said.

"No, you just didn't want to take the risks I was willing to. And it didn't pan out the way I had hoped, now, did it?"

"You aren't blaming yourself for the death of the crew, are you?" the XO asked as they walked back to the boat. Autumn just nodded.

"Then you're more stupid than I thought."

Autumn looked at him, angry again. She was dealing with her own internal conflicts alongside her physical ones, and he had the nerve to call her stupid.

"You are the only reason we're alive now. Your actions saved us. If we had gone my way, we would all be dead. Instead, some survivors will see port again," he explained.

Autumn felt tears welling up in her eyes. She looked away from him, not wanting him to see them. She felt a hand on her face and looked back. The XO wiped a tear from her cheek. He tried to withdraw his hand, but Autumn held it in place with her own. She saw the bandage on the XO's arm turning red and let go of his hand.

"We have to get you back to the *Blue Jay*," she said and motioned to the COB.

"I'm bringing the XO back to the ship. Can you oversee things here?"

The COB glanced at both of them then nodded. "Yes Ma'am."

* * *

It took hours, but finally, all of the *Titan's* nuclear warheads were loaded onto the *Blue Jay*. The mechanic had to check them all to ensure none was rigged to go off.

Autumn stood on the *Blue Jay's* back looking across the water to the *Titan*. She had given the *Titan's* crew ten minutes to get away even though she knew it would do them no good. She had not only destroyed the *Titan's* props but had damaged the ballast system when the tower fell. Now in the fading light, they were dead in the water.

"That's ten minutes Ma'am. Should we fire?" a voice asked over the radio. The *Blue Jay's* orders had been to find, retrieve the warheads and then destroy the *Titan*. Autumn didn't want to give the order, but she had to. If she disobeyed, Dale would surely kill her mother.

"Fire," was all she said into the walky-talky. Seconds later, a torpedo shot from the *Blue Jay's* side. Its path was short; it dug into the *Titan,* exploding full force. The resulting fire ignited the fuel in the now disarmed missiles, causing a chain reaction of explosions all along the *Titan's* spine. Her middle gave way as the sound of tearing bulkheads filled the air. Fire surrounded the dying ship as she twisted and tore. Autumn couldn't stand it anymore. She let the tears fall as she turned away from her sin, closing her eyes as tight as she could, wishing it would all just go away. She felt a hand lift her chin. She opened her eyes and found herself staring into the XO's face. She didn't care if he saw her cry; she needed to cry, so she rested her head on his good shoulder and sobbed.

"What have I done? They were unarmed, immobile, already sinking, and I shot them." The XO began to pat her hair, which had long ago fallen out of its standard military bun.

"It's okay," he said softly. "You did what you had to." They stayed there, not moving for several minutes, then the radio beeped.

"We're reloaded and ready to dive."

Autumn sighed, "We best get back to it XO," she said, lifting her head off his shoulder.

"Can you do me a favour Ma'am," the XO asked. Autumn nodded. "Call me Frank," Autumn smiled and wiped the moisture from her face. Then she did something she thought she would never do.

"Only if you call me Autumn."

Western South Port Naval Base

Dale didn't need the light from the choppers to confirm the rumours he had heard. The second that it pulled in, he knew. With her markings glowing brightly in the night, there was no better sight for him. Autumn was home. However, once the harbour lights snapped on, his heart sank. The *Blue Jay* was so beaten; it was hard to imagine anyone surviving. He grabbed his phone.

"Hello, yes, get as many ambulances as you have to the South Port yesterday!" He hung up, not waiting for a response. He walked briskly down the pier. Despite her damage, the *Blue Jay* made port easily. Dale was the first up the gang plank and helped three men out of the access hatch. Then the XO came up.

"Frank, what the heck happened?" Dale asked.

"I got shot."

"Is Autumn okay?" Dale thought he saw a flash of something in Frank's eyes, but it was too quick for him to know what.

"Ask her yourself." At that moment, Autumn came up the hatch, supported by the COB. Dale quickly urged the COB away and took over helping Autumn down the gangplank.

"Did you do it?" he asked when they reached the bottom.

Autumn nodded. "More...there's more crew in the engine...and torpedo rooms."

"Don't worry about them. We'll get them." Dale reassured her, then put her onto a stretcher. The paramedics loaded her into the ambulance and drove off. Dale then climbed back up the gangplank and walked to the *Blue Jay's* CON. He only got lost once, which was a record for him on board naval vessels. Once there, he walked up to a console and inserted a flash drive. The screen lit up and displayed the word

COPYING...

Before it finished, however, the lights flickered and sparks erupted from the other side of the room. Then everything went dark.

Breaking Point

Past Crush Depth

La Petite Forchet

Six months later

"Is everything alright, darling? You've barely touched your dinner," Dale inquired after swallowing a big chunk of shrimp.

Autumn sighed and straightened her dress. "I'm fine. I just haven't had much of an appetite since the mission." Autumn hated every moment of this. Dale has used her mother to force Autumn to spend time with him. The dates were everything a girl could ask for, fancy restaurants, elegant parties, the whole shebang, but it was hard to enjoy it when the man you were with had partially signed your death warrant a few months ago.

"Ah, yes. Would you indulge me once again?" Dale continued, "How did you beat *Titan*?" Guilt swirled up inside Autumn; she was repulsed by what she had done. She hadn't even explained those moments to her therapist, and yet had on many occasions been forced to relive them with Dale. She didn't want to relive it again, but she knew for her mother's sake, she had to put up a good front.

"She was a slug. Slow, heavy, vulnerable. A diesel, which only made things easier. My excellent Communications Officer hacked their alarm system and fooled them into thinking they had a deadly carbon monoxide build up..." Autumn continued to explain their efforts, and Dale sat there listening. Being careful to outline the contribution of her crew rather than her own, she had to hand it to him; he had a way of making a girl feel important.

After she finished, Dale straightened himself, "Magnificent. We need to give you another medal. This one for brilliance."

The crew of the *Blue Jay* had already won many medals for their actions, but Autumn had won far more than her share. She now always wore a pin over her heart. The pin was a two-dimensional image of the *Blue Jay* in her damaged state. For her, it was a constant reminder of the pain and suffering of her crew. To others, it was the symbol of the best Captain in the Navy. She didn't want any of the fame. She wanted it all to go away. She rarely slept, and the times she did, it was fitful and filled with nightmares. But it was always there, and she couldn't outrun it.

Dale finished, and they left the restaurant with Autumn's plate barely touched. They climbed into a limo and drove away. Dale wrapped his arm around Autumn; she had half a mind to snap it off, but decided against it.

"Are you sleeping well, my sweet?" he asked, placing his free hand on her knee. That was too much for her, so she pushed his hand away.

"Fine," she lied. "One thing has been nagging me, though."

"And what is that?" Dale asked.

"The *Blue Jay*. How bad was the damage, and will she ever sail again?" Autumn would hate to see the *Blue Jay* scrapped or turned into a museum. It deserved to sail until it fell apart.

"The damage was extensive. It had multiple cracks in its frame, and the controls were heavily damaged. It was a miracle it survived some of the manoeuvres you pulled. They only recently got it dry docked," Dale explained.

Autumn frowned. Yet another piece of information to show how reckless she had been. Although not one person on board the boat mentioned it, she felt she hadn't made the best decisions during the mission.

"How bad were the cracks?" she asked, her voice sounding so distant that it was like another person had joined the conversation.

"Have a look for yourself," Dale said, pointing out the window.

Autumn hadn't even noticed the limo stopping, but they were parked in front of the gates to dry dock number four. She wasn't sure if she wanted to see the ship, but she knew that Dale wanted her to. She opened the door and climbed out. Dale closed it behind them. She walked in and her heart nearly stopped. Her face must have drained of colour because Dale gave her a gentle hug.

"I know. Come, let's walk around."

They moved closer. The *Blue Jay* looked miserable. Her markings weren't lit, and she was propped up on metal supports. She looked out of place, her bow not even pointing towards the sea, where she belonged. As Autumn walked towards the stern, she ran her hand across the once smooth skin. It was scraped, crumpled and scarred across the entire length of the ship. Guilt assaulted Autumn as she saw a gaping hole where the crew's quarters were. She knew some of the families of the men who had died in there, and the others wasted no time getting to know her.

At the *Blue Jay's* stern, Autumn was given her first look at the part of the ship that she had relied on so heavily. The props were slightly bent, but nothing serious. Its control surfaces were another story. She knew the upper rudder was damaged, but nothing like the bottom one. It must have taken a huge beating when the *Blue Jay* slid on the sea floor. The pitch control had been dented but not that badly, relatively speaking.

Autumn held back tears as she spoke. "All this damage, and she still ran like she was new. Remind me to thank the designers."

"Yes, many people were shocked to find the damage," someone said behind them. Autumn turned to find a man covered in grease walking up to them.

"Excuse me, but this is a private viewing of the vessel," Dale stated firmly. The man held his hands up and backed away, disappearing into a building.

"What did you do that for? He only wanted to meet the West's newest celebrity." Autumn knew it sounded self-centred, but she couldn't let the man go to jail for interrupting.

"Perhaps you're right. Still, I didn't want you to be disturbed. It's your moment with your ship." Dale said, shrugging his shoulders.

"It's not my ship anymore," Autumn said, letting regret fill her voice. "What will happen to her?"

"It'll be repaired and put back into service," Dale responded and slipped his hand onto Autumn's lower back. "But she needs a Captain."

"Who will take the position?" Autumn asked.

"I thought you would like to."

"Dale, the ship will be ready to sail before I am. Besides, I don't think I can." Autumn wanted nothing more than to command the *Blue Jay* again, but knew it was impractical.

"Doesn't matter. It's your ship; it stays in port until you're ready to sail. If you never are, then the *Blue Jay* never will be either. No Captain can bring out its full potential like you can, and I need its full potential. As long as your commission stays active, you'll command it," Dale said, flatteringly.

Autumn felt herself blush. "Well, that's very nice of you, but she deserves to sail. Perhaps–"

"Autumn, honey. You aren't listening to me. It's yours. If you just want to go for a cruise across the bay, you can. You'll get to hand-pick the crew. The whole thing is yours; I'll only ask that you be ready to defend the ports should the East try anything," Dale said.

Autumn was shocked. Dale's gifts were always extravagant: beautiful dresses and expensive jewelry. She never wanted any of them, and she didn't want this one either. After being through hell and back, the *Blue Jay* deserved more than becoming a personal watercraft. But at least if it was hers and it would never get turned into something worse. She put on her best fake smile.

"Thank you so much," she said, hiding her resentment perfectly.

"You deserve it as much as it deserves you," Dale said affectionately. "Shall I bring you home?" Autumn nodded and let him escort her out of the yard, her head resting on his shoulders.

Past Crush Depth

176 Catwalk Drive

Thunder cracked across the sky. Autumn stood, unable to look away as the Titan burned. She could hear the screams of men. The bodies of her crew floated around her. The Titan wouldn't sink; it just stayed up, burning, almost hollering out in pain as it was tortured, unable to die. Then blackness filled Autumn's eyes, and when it cleared, she was left standing on the Titan's back. Fire burned all around the blood-stained deck, and there were dismembered bodies everywhere. Autumn was pointing her gun at the XO of the Titan and swung it off to shoot a crew member, but instead, she shot herself.

Autumn woke up in a cold sweat, her heart racing. She looked over at her clock. 1:00 AM. She had gotten half an hour of sleep. Pretty good. She turned on her bedside lamp and threw off her covers. She grabbed her robe and made her way to her kitchen. She looked at the picture of her, Frank and the COB on her fridge. They had attended a dinner together and received awards for their actions. Dale had taken the picture. She sighed and reached for a glass when she heard a knock at the door. Puzzled, she left the glass and went to the door. When she opened it, she felt her heart slow to an almost normal speed.

"Frank?" she said stupidly. She hadn't seen him since the dinner and wasn't expecting to for a long time.

"Hello, Autumn. May I come in?" Frank asked. He was wearing black track pants with a red strip down the side and a standard issue Nava P.T. shirt. He looked sweaty like he had just been running, but he wasn't short of breath.

"Yes, of course," she responded, moving out of the doorway to let him in. "Have a seat. Make yourself at home. Would you like a drink? Tea, water...whiskey?"

"A whiskey sounds good," Frank answered casually. Of course, the whiskey sounded good. She was sure that the reason he was here was the same reason she was awake. Feeling a bit stupid, she turned to the small bar in the corner of the living room, pulling out two crystal glasses with the *Blue Jay* elaborately engraved on them. She had been given all sorts of memorabilia, constant reminders of the mission.

"I saw the *Blue Jay* today," Autumn said, as she poured the whiskey.

"How'd she look?" Frank asked, accepting the glass.

"Not good. It was a miracle that we made it back."

"Then we better start calling you the Miracle Captain," Frank laughed.

"Don't you dare. I already have enough fame to deal with," Autumn was laughing as well.

"Ah, yes. The heroic Captain of the *Blue Jay*, glasses and all," he joked, pointing to his untouched glass of whiskey.

"Is that all you came here for? To tease me about this mess?" Autumn asked, taking a small sip from her glass.

"Well, I'll admit that your apartment could be cleaner..." Autumn nearly spat her drink out laughing. It was true she was not the best housekeeper, but the way he said it...

"Okay, seriously," Autumn said after regaining her composure. "What's on your mind?"

"Couldn't sleep," Frank sighed. Autumn shook her head, and it was enough to prompt Frank to continue. "Ever since the dinner, I haven't been able to get you off my mind."

"Well, I don't think any of the crew has been able to get that mission out of their minds," Autumn said, taking another sip of whiskey.

"No, Autumn. You. I haven't been able to get *you* off my mind." The whiskey caught in Autumn's throat. "I love you." Autumn swallowed the burning liquid and proceeded to drain her glass. She had feelings for him in the past, but knew it wouldn't work out. Even if she allowed herself to love him, Dale would see to it that he died, one horrible way or another.

"Frank I..."

"No. Don't say a thing. I knew the truth when I came here. You're dating Dale. I just needed you to know," Frank said, and placed his glass on the coffee table between them.

"It's not that, Frank. I don't want to date him; I just have to," Autumn said, shyly. She was convinced that Frank wouldn't understand.

"Your mother?" he asked. Autumn looked at him, surprised. "You mentioned Dale killing off our loved ones if we didn't complete the mission. I heard your mother is in the hospital." Autumn couldn't say anything. She just nodded. Had she said that? There was a blank spot in her memory from some point in the mission around where she passed out. She might have said something, or was he following her?

"I understand," Frank said and stood up.

"I would much rather love you," Autumn blurted out, and immediately hated herself for it.

"No, you wouldn't. I blamed you for my demotion, and I have been nothing but disrespectful the past year. And I still would be if not for that mission. You deserve better, Autumn. If you must settle for Dale, then so be it. But if you can, find someone who deserves you," Frank stated, staring her right in the eyes. "Thanks for the drink. I can see myself out."

Frank left, leaving Autumn alone in her living room. Her hands shook as she placed her glass on the coffee table. *Doesn't deserve me?* She thought. The man had been a pain, but people change. The whole trip back, he had been nothing but respectful and the perfect XO. If anything, it was she who didn't deserve him.

Seaside Air Force Base

Autumn opened the door to her government-issued sports car and climbed out. She resented being the government's dress-up girl. The car she used even had the *Blue Jay's* markings on it. Dale had requested that she use her *Blue Jay-themed* belongings as much as possible. She found it embarrassing. Both she and the *Blue Jay* were being shown off like prized possessions. Either way, she had to live with it now.

She walked to the administration desk and saluted the young officer behind it. Along with her awards, Autumn had received a large promotion to Master Captain. It was the first time anyone had had this rank in years. It basically meant that she was still commanding a vessel, but everyone in the military was obliged to salute her and respect her as a superior. Her rank even superseded that of the Navy Master.

"No need for the I.D. Ma'am," the young officer said as Autumn reached for her I.D.

"And what if I'm a spy?" she asked. The young officer gave her a look and then understood. There was no reason for changing the protocol for her.

"Very well, Ma'am. May I see your I.D, please?" Autumn handed him the card, and she got it back quickly.

"Looking for anyone, or just visiting?" the young man asked.

"I'm looking for the *Shredder*," Autumn replied, and the man smiled.

"She's just by the maintenance hangar. They finally fixed the damage your gun did."

"No secrets anywhere," Autumn laughed.

"Watch yourself there, Ma'am. Word is the *Shredder's* Captain still hasn't forgiven you." Autumn nodded, thanked the young man for his help and made her way to the tarmac. When she reached the *Shredder,* she stood there admiring it and the fresh coat of blue matte paint on its nose. But the painting crew hadn't finished their job. There were still burn marks along the wings from when it helped out the *Blue Jay* with the escort problem. It almost looked comical. She took a deep breath and walked up the ramp extending from the plane's belly.

Once onboard, she walked along the metal walkway toward the Captain's quarters; her heels clanking on the metal. She got some sideways looks from the crew, but they saluted when needed. She reached Captain James's door and knocked briskly.

"Come in," a distracted voice called. Autumn opened the door and walked in. The Captain gave her a withering look. "Get off my aircraft."

"I'm going to overlook that indiscretion. I am your Superior now, remember that," Autumn stated firmly. The Captain frowned, evidently just noticing her rank slip-ons.

"Of course, Ma'am. I apologize. Welcome aboard the *Shredder.* To what do I owe the pleasure?" The sarcasm in James's voice was as clear as water in a pool.

"I am here for two reasons. First, I have to thank you for your assistance in the *Blue Jay's* mission. Without the *Shredder,* we surely would have perished. The second reason I am here is to apologize. I should never have fired on your aircraft. I know that if anyone took a shot like that at the *Blue*

Jay I would have personally blown them to pieces. However, know that you didn't leave me much choice. Your disregard for protocol in that situation is what brought about the damage to your plane, not my misjudgment," Autumn stated. James was no longer looking her in the eye. "I am not here under orders. I am here of my own accord. With that, I will not disturb you any longer." Autumn turned on her heels and was about to step off when James piped up behind her.

"This impressed me."

Autumn looked back at him. He had turned a computer monitor around to show an image of the *Blue Jay* pulling around one of the *Titan's* escorts and the *Shredder's* torpedo plowing into the escort, knocking the *Blue Jay* from view. Autumn sighed.

"It was remarkable ship handling. Is it true that you had a head injury?"

"Yes. I hit my head multiple times during the mission," Autumn said quietly.

"Come, let us walk," James suggested. Autumn was a little surprised. Just a minute ago, all the Captain wanted was for her off his aircraft, and now he wanted to show it off to her? She complied, and they walked to the bridge.

"Captain on the bridge," someone said, and everyone turned and saluted. James saluted as well, facing Autumn. She returned the salutes, and then another woman walked up to James. Autumn was puzzled. She couldn't imagine James letting any women on board his gunship.

"This is my wife," James explained. Autumn was disgusted. His wife was wearing the skimpiest outfit and was hanging off him like some sort of accessory—a prize rather than a human being. Autumn shook her head.

"I best get going," she said coldly. James nodded, and Autumn left. She was halfway down the ramp when she heard someone running up behind her. She turned to see James's wife.

"Wait up!" she called. "Master Captain Gayle? Captain of the *Blue Jay*?"

"Yes. May I help you?" Autumn asked.

"My name's Debra. I'm a huge fan," the woman said, panting a little from her run. Autumn was now really confused. She had shot this woman's husband's plane, and now she was a fan.

"Nice to meet you, Debra. What can I do for you?" Autumn extended her hand, and Debra took it eagerly.

"Just a conversation. I have watched the radar footage from the *Shredder* hundreds of times and have some questions," Debra answered. Autumn didn't want to relive the mission, but she wouldn't discourage this young lady, particularly not when she was married to James.

"I would be happy to answer them," Autumn said, and Debra's face lit up.

"Really? Okay first. Did you plan everything, or was it all instinct?"

"We planned a lot, but our defensive actions were instinctive."

"Wow. Did you know the extent of the damage to your sub?" Debra asked, sounding more and more like a groupie.

"No. And, to be honest, I'm glad I didn't. All I knew was that we had a contained radiation leak, that the controls worked, most of the crew was dead, and that we had contained flooding." Debra watched Autumn as she explained her answer as if her life depended on it. Her last question struck Autumn hard.

"So, after the mission, you started to date the Leader of the West. Had the mission made you realize that he was worth going out with, or is there someone else?"

Autumn wasn't sure what to do. Tell the truth, or lie? The truth could come back and hurt her, but so could the lie. She sighed and answered. "The mission changed how I looked at things. I started thinking about my future and what better person than Dale himself."

Debra smiled. "That's so..." Debra hung onto her words but never continued. Autumn was worried she would call her on her lie, but she didn't. She just looked back at the *Shredder,* whose engine was beginning to spool up. "I should get back."

"Debra, can I ask you something?" Autumn said quickly before the woman ran off.

"Sure."

"Why do you let him dress you up and parade you around like a prize?" Autumn inquired.

"I don't have much of a choice. I am his after all. That's why I'm such a fan. You are like a symbol of hope. Showing that women can be equal to men, if not better. You beat the *Titan.* Not a man. You," Debra explained.

"Stand up for yourself, Debra. We aren't any man's property. We're a luxury they don't always deserve," Autumn said, handing Debra a card with her contact information on it. "Call me if you need anything."

Debra's smile grew, and she nodded before heading back to the *Shredder.*

Autumn was about to climb into her car when an ear-splitting shriek filled the air. She looked behind her as a completely black aircraft climbed from the runway. She knew it from the newspapers. The *Dagger,* designed for nothing but sinking ships. The thought made her shiver. Dale now had one more thing to hold over her–the destruction of the *Blue Jay.*

Past Crush Depth

596421 Southwest Boulevard

Autumn sighed. She had been watching the door to Frank's house for the past half hour, but he was nowhere to be found. She was trying to sort things out in her mind, the feelings turning inside her. She knew one thing for certain, though: she had feelings for Frank. She wasn't sure if she wanted to talk to Frank or just see him, but if she didn't want to be seen, she shouldn't have taken her *Blue Jay* car. She decided that it was best to leave and reached for the ignition button when a rap on the window startled her.

"God damn it, Frank. You nearly gave me a heart attack," Autumn said, rolling the window down.

"Sorry," Frank chuckled. "Your spying needs work. I spotted your car four blocks down. Is there something you need?"

Autumn searched her mind for a proper reason but found none. She tried to fabricate a response but came up empty. She hadn't thought this through; she had no reason to be here, except one, to see him.

"Just wanted to see if you wanted to go for a drive. My car's got some kick," Autumn said, trying to sound cool, and failing. Frank just laughed.

"Alright, let's see what you can do,"

Autumn smiled as Frank slid in. She pressed the ignition button. The car's computer beeped in acknowledgment. Then blue light ran across the car from front to back along the now iconic *Blue Jay* marking. She shifted into drive and stomped on the accelerator. The machine sank into its suspension and bolted. Autumn steered into a nearby parking lot. She put the car into a doughnut before doing a backward slalom around the lampposts. The car never even protested. It went along with whatever Autumn wanted. She powered onto a dirt road and up a hill. They crested, the car gaining air as it did so. The suspension on the vehicle was so good that they were barely bumped around inside. Eventually, she parked it on a ledge overlooking the city lights.

"That does have some kick. What kind of engine is in this thing?" Frank asked.

Autumn just shrugged. "I don't know. Big," she replied. "How has therapy been?"

"Fine. Getting better every day. You?"

"Same. Do you think you could ever serve on board the *Blue Jay* again?" Autumn asked. She decided it was no use to beat around the bush. She had a question, and she needed an answer.

"Maybe. I don't know," Frank responded. "Why?"

"They're putting me back in command of her," Autumn said.

"Good for you. Are you going to be able to do it, mentally?" Frank asked.

"I don't know, and that's what I want to ask you. Could you be my XO again? I need someone I trust on the bridge."

"Autumn, you don't want me as XO. Before that mission, I was nothing but a problem for you. If not for the mission, I still would be," Frank looked out the window at the lights below.

"We made it back, didn't we? Besides, you were the best XO on the home trip," Autumn pushed. She didn't want to tell him the real reason she wanted him onboard. She did want someone she could trust, but she also wanted an excuse to be near him. If he were onboard, they would be forced to spend time together, and she could sort out her feelings and maybe make something of them. Out where Dale couldn't hurt her.

"You truly want me as your XO?" Frank asked.

"Yes. But only if you can. I don't want you doing anything you can't do," Autumn said.

"Alright. I'll do it. But I'm gone if I start becoming a problem, understood?"

Autumn laughed. "Sure thing. Now, let's tear up some dirt." With a nod of agreement from Frank, she threw the car into gear and sped down the path, leaving a plume of dust behind.

Past Crush Depth

Western South Port Naval Base

Autumn's heart leapt with joy when she saw the *Blue Jay*. No longer beaten, no longer crippled, and back in the water where she belonged. The repair crew had done an excellent job. If she didn't know better, she would have said that the ship had never seen combat.

"Why don't you climb aboard?" Dale offered. Autumn nodded, and she, Dale and Frank climbed the gangplank. They walked to the bridge, and Autumn gasped. It had been completely redesigned. The only things that looked the same were the helm controls. All the displays were holographic, each console redesigned for maximum efficiency and her chair was surrounded by two wrap-around displays.

"It was already the most advanced ship in the fleet. Why all this?" Autumn asked.

"Why not. We had the opportunity, so we ran with it," Dale explained. "A lot of this is to fix problems that you had on the last mission. The ship can now be crewed by two people in the bridge, engine room, and weapons room." Autumn shook her head. He was already planning to sacrifice the majority of the *Blue Jay's* new crew to rule the world. Typical.

"Captain has the bridge," Frank said and sat down in his chair, which also had a wraparound display. Autumn smiled and took her seat.

"Cast off," she ordered. Instantly, a side camera view flew onto her display, showing her exactly what she needed. So far, she was impressed. Once out of the harbour, Autumn began to experiment with her display. It was weird. Her therapist had said that this might be difficult, but she was happy. Seeing the *Blue Jay* repaired, the life breathed back into her was a rush. Even her mother was starting to recover. Although nothing would ever be the same, Autumn's life was starting to get back on track. She swiped the display and brought up a 3D model of the *Blue Jay*. This image sent streaks of guilt through her. The diagram displayed each compartment with its status. It also showed the reactor cooling lines. She wasn't sure exactly why this made her feel guilty, but it did. She dismissed the image and sighed heavily.

"Are you all right, honey?" Dale asked. Autumn sat up in her chair.

"Fine, just a flashback, nothing serious."

Dale nodded, "Don't push yourself. Do you want to sail her?"

Autumn sighed again. She wasn't sure if she did, but it was a good idea to face everything that had happened during the mission, and there was no time like the present. She stood up, and the wrap-around display slid apart to allow her to leave without walking through the hologram. The Helmsman stepped aside, and Autumn took a seat in front of the controls.

"Let's see how I do with undamaged controls," Autumn joked. The Helmsmen leaned over and began to explain the controls. "I sailed as a Helmsman for years."

"Sorry, Ma'am, force of habit," the Helmsman replied.

"Don't worry. I would be worried if I were in your shoes," Autumn said softly.

"Take her away, sweetie," Dale encouraged. Autumn nodded and pushed the throttles forward. Instantly, she felt the uninterrupted power of the *Blue Jay*, the same power that had saved her and the surviving crew, the same power that she loved so much. She checked her depth below the keel display. The harbour was built so that the water gained depth rapidly upon exiting the break walls. This permitted submarines to wait in hiding if the enemy was getting close. As a result, there would be plenty of room for what she was going to do. She smiled and threw the controls to the left. The *Blue Jay* rolled onto her side, and Autumn pulled her around in a circle before levelling off and diving. She watched the depth gauge and noticed a small display that showed sonar information. At about 50 feet above the sea floor, Autumn pulled the bow up, and a few seconds later, the *Blue Jay* broke the surface of the water, like a whale breaching. The bridge was silent except for the clicking of the displays.

"Holy..." the Helmsman mumbled.

"Bet you didn't know she could do that," Autumn chuckled. Dale rested his hand on her shoulder.

"How does she handle?"

"Like brand new. You couldn't have done a better job," Autumn said. She looked up and smiled at him. She hated it, but she had to keep up appearances for her mother's sake.

"There's a tanker out there, old, decrepit, due to be destroyed. They know you can drive, now show them how you can command," Dale suggested.

"My pleasure," Autumn agreed and changed seats once again. She slid the display back into place and then ordered, "All ahead flank, turn heading one-six-seven degrees." The ship began a slow turn towards the tanker. "She can take a beating. I want tight turns," Autumn stated enthusiastically. The turn suddenly increased, and they were soon on the new heading. "That's more like it." Autumn was having fun; for the first time in months, she was having fun! She belonged on the bridge of the *Blue Jay*. The target soon became outlined in red on the window display.

"We have a firing solution, Ma'am," Frank said. Autumn was glad to have Frank with her. Although the bridge looked different, it was still nice to have a friend.

"Fire, Helm brings us up, I want to see smoke," Autumn ordered and chuckled. The *Blue Jay* surfaced just as its torpedo detonated. The old tanker erupted into flames and began to sink rapidly; the sound of tearing bulkheads filled the bridge. Autumn's mind flashed back to the defenceless *Titan,* burning, dying. She felt tears well up as pangs of guilt stabbed at her.

"Ma'am, are you alright?" Frank asked. Autumn felt the first tear fall. "Ma'am?" Frank was so formal on the bridge. It helped, but wasn't enough to keep her from crying. She stood up, spreading the display.

"XO, you have the CON," she said and walked out the door. Dale followed.

"Autumn, sweetie, it's okay. Maybe that was too much." Autumn just kept crying. She walked to her quarters, then turned and accepted his embrace. Resting her head on his shoulder, letting him pat her hair. This, however, only made her cry even more.

* * *

Autumn was standing on the back of the *Blue Jay* with no lights, nothing but darkness. Not even the ship's markings were lit. It was all for a display at the military demonstration. The return of the mighty *Blue Jay* and her Captain. Autumn had been kicking herself for how she had behaved on the bridge earlier, even though her therapist stated it was only normal. She was wrenched from her thoughts when a loud booming voice came from the shore.

"Ladies and Gentlemen! We are proud to present to you your favourite Captain, the one who saved the lives of many crews and has taken the worst the East can throw at her, Master Captain Autumn Gayle!" Cheers rose from the crowd on the shore as a spotlight landed on Autumn. She forced a smile and waved. "Now for the one ship you have all been waiting to see, the newly rebuilt *BLUE JAY!*" the voice called. With that, Autumn stomped her foot, and the markings on the ship's side came to life. Blue light snaked its way from the stern to the bow, where it swirled into the now iconic *Blue Jay* symbol. Autumn couldn't believe it; the crowd was going wild for this.

"This Captain and ship are the symbols of Western superiority!" a new voice boomed. "They will bring peace to our world with the help of the *Shredder...*" At that moment, the *Shredder* flew overhead, "...*the Dagger...*" The *Shredder* was followed by the ship-killing *Dagger,* and then a submarine surfaced off the *Blue Jay's* port side. "...and the *Arrow Head.* Together, these ships and aircraft will escort peacekeepers to the East where they will sign a peace treaty to forever end the war between hemispheres!"

The crowd went nuts, but Autumn felt her stomach twist into a knot. It didn't make sense. Dale wanted nothing but power. Peace with the East would mean he would never have full control unless he had something else planned. That suspicion made Autumn very uneasy, and as the rest of the show went on, she retreated below deck.

"COB! Get the XO to my quarters in five minutes," she ordered, and then walked into her quarters. The room was small but nice. It was, thankfully, plain white with no *Blue Jay* markings anywhere. It was a peaceful place. It had a small wooden table with a built-in computer in the far corner and a good-sized bunk in another corner. The rest of the room consisted of an eating table, some chairs, and a storage closet.

"Come in," Autumn said, as a knock came at the door. Frank stepped in and closed the door behind him. He had a worried look on his face. "I take it you heard about our orders?" she asked. Frank just nodded. Autumn opened a cupboard and pulled out two glasses and a bottle of whiskey.

"They worry me," Frank said, taking a glass.

"Me too. Not only the concept, but why send escorts?" Autumn said, sitting down in a chair at the table, and motioning for Frank to do the same.

"Keep us safe?" Frank suggested.

"No, we can outrun the *Arrowhead,* meaning we would have to be travelling slower so she could keep up, and that would put both ships at risk. Plus, the aircraft would be constantly circling, giving away our position," Autumn stated, taking a big slug of whiskey. The effects of her flashback earlier hadn't fully worn off yet.

"Dale has something planned, and it's not peace," Frank said.

"Look, Frank, I have to follow orders, but I can't make you do this. If you want out, then walk off this boat as soon as we dock, okay?" Autumn stated.

Frank shook his head. "I'm in this all the way. If you go, then I go."

Autumn smiled. "Thank you, that means a lot."

"You think about them a lot, don't you?" Frank asked, after a long moment of silence.

"Who?"

"The crew, more than I do," Frank replied.

"I doubt that. Why do you ask?" Autumn inquired.

"Because every time I visit, we always drink something. I barely touch my glass while you take two or three," Frank explained. Autumn sighed. He was right. "You can't keep blaming yourself for that mission, Autumn. You are the reason we're home, you're the reason that the West still exists! Without you, the world as we know it would be dead. The *Blue Jay* would be sitting on the bottom of the ocean, and I would never have had the privilege of loving you." Autumn flinched. He still loved her, even after she had flirted with Dale right in front of him, even after acknowledging the fact that it would never work out.

"Frank I..."

"Autumn, you are amazing, stubborn but amazing. You know that. If I were in your shoes, I would have killed myself by now," Frank continued. Autumn felt like her heart was being ripped open. She knew she loved him, but her practical side fought against it, and neither side was winning. Autumn quickly tried to change to subject.

"What do you think our chances of making it back are?"

"With you? Anything's possible. I think the *Blue Jay* will make it back, but I doubt the rest will," Frank said.

Autumn shook her head, "I don't want to do this."

"No one does. It's a horrible job," Frank encouraged. "If I could, I would take your place." Autumn was done with turmoil. She didn't care anymore. She leaned over and kissed Frank.

Western Defence Command

"Why on earth would I surrender?" the Commander of the Eastern world asked Dale. Dale motioned for an operator, and images of the *Blue Jay* and her escorts leaving port appeared.

"Do you recognize those markings?" Dale asked.

"Should I?"

"That's the ship that took out the *Titan*," Dale explained. There was a slight shift in the Eastern Commander's face.

"I don't see your point. We are far superior to the West. The loss of the *Titan* was a minor setback. You got lucky."

"Really? Because that ship—with barely any crew left—defeated your attempt to overthrow us completely."

"I repeat, you got lucky. I mean, you put a woman in charge of a sub! That in itself is an embarrassment. I could win this by just letting you come to me. Your ships come in, die, and suddenly, your Navy is depleted," the Eastern Leader chuckled. Dale was furious.

"Perhaps I didn't make myself clear. The ship you should be truly afraid of is the *Blue Jay*, but the ship she is escorting is by far more dangerous to you. It carries the warheads taken from the *Titan*. If you don't surrender before they reach your shores, those ships have orders to fire at your Parliament." Dale stated.

"You wouldn't dare risk that. We have a counterattack."

"If that were true, you would have made another attempt by now, or you're just plain stupid to pass up the opportunity," Dale said, now mocking the East.

"You risk losing everything over this attack!" the Eastern Leader snapped.

"No more than you. Surrender or face the consequences," Dale cut the call, and the screen went blank. He then looked at a display that had a series of red dots on a map. These were the *Arrowhead's* true targets. They were major military bases in the East. If destroyed, the Eastern military would be severely crippled, and they would be forced to surrender. Of course, Dale didn't truly want to fire any nukes. It was too risky. The plan was that the threat of the nuke detonating in such a populated area as the Capital, plus the threat of the *Blue Jay*, would be enough to force the East into submission. That's why he had sent Autumn on this mission. Her presence would maximize the effect of the *Blue Jay*.

"Sir," someone called behind him. Dale turned to see a young aide rushing up to him.

"Yes?"

"You asked me to keep an eye on the condition of Master Captain Gayle's mother," the aide stated, clearly uncomfortable. "There has been a development."

"What kind of development?" Dale asked.

"She's taken a turn for the worse. The doctors aren't sure she'll make it," the aide said. Dale grabbed his sidearm and shot the aide in the foot. The man hollered in pain, and the entire room fell silent. Dale's mind was racing.

The only reason Autumn spent time with him was because of her mother. If that woman died, Dale would lose Autumn forever.

"Tell the doctors they had better keep that woman alive! Do you understand me? I want her alive!"

Western Attack Submarine *Blue Jay*

"I most certainly will not! A tight formation gives us a significant advantage in battle," the Captain of the *Arrowhead* yelled over the radio. Autumn rolled her eyes. She had been arguing with this man for half an hour now and was fed up. She glanced at Frank, who wouldn't look at her. Things had been tense since she'd kissed him. She had made a mistake. Frank knew it wouldn't work out between them, and she just added insult to injury with that action. She grabbed the microphone.

"Look, Buster. I brought down four subs with one torpedo because they were in a tight formation."

"Right. And I was wearing a pink dress yesterday," the Captain mocked.

"You blow one up, the resulting shockwave jams the controls of the two other subs. One of the damaged subs hits another sub, and the other hits the sea floor. Basically, if you blow up right now, the *Blue Jay* becomes crippled. If we blow up, you sink. So back off or we leave you in our baffles," Autumn snapped. She caught a smile from the COB as she spoke. "Have you forgotten who you are talking to?"

"Of course not. We'll loosen the formation," the Captain spat, "Anything else?"

"Are your ship and crew presentable?" Autumn asked.

"Come check them yourself. They are perfectly fine."

"That's what I'm afraid of. I want a full ceremonial uniform, swords, and everything," Autumn said. "I'll be there in ten, surface and prepare to receive." With that, Autumn ended the transmission. "XO, you have the CON." Just as Autumn was about to leave, Frank grabbed her by the arm.

"You aren't going there by yourself, are you?" he asked.

"That was the plan."

"Ma'am, I don't think that's a good Idea. You are a woman." His words cut deep. "Ma'am, the Captain has a reputation."

"Then it's a good thing I have my sword," Autumn growled and left the bridge. She walked to the ladder and climbed onto the *Blue Jay's* back. She stopped momentarily to breathe in the fresh sea air. This inspection may have been unnecessary, and the order for the officers onboard to wear their ceremonial swords was definitely overkill, but it would get her message across. The *Arrowhead* was under her direction, not the other way around.

The ship in question surfaced, and she walked across the gangplank. The fact that the Captain didn't meet her upon boarding did not escape Autumn. She shook her head at the display of disrespect. She made it below deck as the *Arrowhead* began to submerge once again, escaping to the depths of the sea.

It took time, but eventually Autumn had inspected all of the *Arrowhead*. Something was out of place. Cargo holds were blocked by "malfunctioning doors". It seemed odd that a ship like this would be sailing with such a problem, considering all the food was commonly stored in the cargo hold. Even more so that she was not notified of the ship's deficiency before departure. By the time Autumn had reached the bridge, she had already shot down multiple sexual advances from the crew, but nothing would prepare her for what she found on the bridge. When she walked in, she stopped dead in her tracks. The Captain was not what she had been expecting; he was fat, really fat, and smoking a large cigar.

"Welcome aboard, Master Captain," he said politely, "I trust you find the ship in good order?"

"Aside from behaviour issues from the crew and a few doors, the ship is indeed in good order," Autumn replied, walking around the bridge. It was far less advanced than the *Blue Jay,* with a standard liquid plasma display and analog instruments.

"Ah, yes. Well, there have been very few females on board," the Captain said. The way he said females sent a chill down Autumn's spine. Two crew members grabbed Autumn by the arms, holding her in place. One of the men ripped her tunic off and threw her gun away. She knew then that she was in trouble. The Captain drew his sword. "There's a price to pay for that." The Captain rested his sword on Autumn's shoulder, running it down across the fabric of her shirt until it reached her waist.

"Being away at sea..." the *Arrowhead's* Captain slipped the sword under the lowest button on Autumn's shirt, and with a quick twist, the button popped free. Landing with an audible *clink* in the silent bridge, "...has its disadvantages." Another button popped as the sword travelled upwards. The usual blunt ceremonial weapon had been sharpened. Making Autumn wonder how many women had been subjected to his *hospitality.*

"You—" Autumn began, but was cut off as the Captain slapped her across the face.

"Don't speak unless told to!" he shouted. Then, as if to accent his control over her, he popped another button on her shirt to the floor. Each *clink* of her shirt buttons hitting the floor seemed louder than the last. It was made worse by the knowledge that Autumn only had two buttons left.

"Sir, the *Blue Jay's* wondering when their Captain will be ready to return," someone asked.

"Tell them she's still performing *inspections*," the Captain laughed as he cut another button free, exposing Autumn's plain white bra. Autumn looked frantically for an escape, finally managing to elbow one of the men holding her and pull the knife hidden in a sheath on the back of her belt, bashing its hilt on the other man's head. The man cried out in pain as she blocked the attack from the Captain. She was still nowhere near clear. She was now in a sword fight with a tactical knife. The Captain definitely had training with his weapon despite the close quarters they were in. She blocked the downward track of the blade with her weapon but lost her balance and stumbled backward. She felt herself losing control as she continued to back towards the controls. The Captain slashed at her left bra strap, cutting the strap and flesh around it. What was left holding Autumn's shirt together fell apart, fully exposing her. She turned and threw the Helmsman out of his seat, then she slammed the controls down and to the left, putting the *Arrowhead* into a spiralling dive away from the *Blue Jay*. This move also knocked some of the crew from their feet. However, she hadn't really dealt with the Helmsman. The now disgruntled man grabbed her and held her while another man delivered two quick punches to her abdomen, causing her to drop her knife

"Now, boys, don't break her. We still want to use that body," the Captain warned, and the men released Autumn. She scrambled for her blade, but before she could reach it, she felt a blade slash down her spine. It was a painful cut, and her bra fell from her chest. Then, just as her hand reached her only weapon, the Helmsman stomped his foot on it.

Damn it, Autumn thought to herself. The Captain grabbed her and pinned her against a periscope, his blade to her throat. She felt handcuffs being placed around her wrist which were now held above her head exposing her naked breasts to the crew of men. She had never felt so helpless in her entire life. Exposed, vulnerable, at the mercy of these merciless men. She decided that she wasn't going down yet. She tried to free herself from the cuffs, but to no avail.

"Looks like we've got ourselves a fighter boys!" the Captain boasted.

"You'll never get away with this!" Autumn yelled, but she knew she had lost. A blindfold was placed over her eyes.

"I think we will," the Captain said, grabbing her left breast. Autumn squirmed, trying to get away from the fat man's touch, but she couldn't. The bridge was silent now, the tension high. Autumn wondered how many of these men would have their way with her, probably all of them. Then she heard the distinctive click of the hammer of a gun. The Captain released Autumn's breast quickly. Obviously, he was as surprised by this sound as Autumn was.

"Step away from my Captain and put your hands on your head," Frank ordered. Autumn partially yelled out in joy, but also felt her face turning red from embarrassment. She hated the idea of anyone seeing her like this, especially Frank.

"Why would we do that? I'm sure you'd like to join in," the Captain proposed.

"Perhaps I didn't make myself clear. Back away," Frank stated sternly.

"Or what?" the Captain asked.

"The *Blue Jay* is listening in. They hear something they don't like, and we're all on the bottom of the ocean," Frank replied.

"The *Arrowhead* can take a few hits. I'm not concerned."

"They're aiming at her flaw, Captain."

Autumn was taken aback by this. She wasn't aware there was a major flaw in the *Arrowhead*.

"You wouldn't dare," the Captain's voice was now more fretful.

"We shot the *Shredder*," Frank persisted. There was a crash of metal, and Autumn's hands fell free. She instantly pulled her tattered shirt over her chest, and soon the blindfold had been lifted. Once her eyes adjusted to the light, she saw it was just Frank there, no one else. The courage he showed to come alone baffled Autumn. She moved close to Frank desperate for someone who felt safe to her.

"I trust we won't have any further problems?" Frank stated.

"Get off my ship," the Captain spat. With that, Frank led Autumn towards the stern of the *Arrowhead*. They climbed up a ladder and into a transfer sub from the *Blue Jay*. The sub was small, you couldn't fit more than five people inside it, with a glass-dome window making up her entire bow. The controls and two wooden benches lined the walls of the cabin. Autumn sat down at the back of one of the benches, facing away from Frank. The one thing she had tried to so hard to avoid in her career had almost happened. If not for Frank, it would have, she was sure of that. But for Frank, she wouldn't be able to continue commanding the *Blue Jay*. She felt a hand on her shoulder and jumped.

"It's okay, it's just me," Frank said, sitting down on the bench behind her. Autumn couldn't bring herself to face him. She felt helpless, lost, angry, and weak. She felt a cold, burning cloth on the cut on her back as Frank cleaned it, with what she assumed to be alcohol.

"My God, you're trembling," Frank remarked as he continued to dress her wound. Autumn couldn't even speak; his touch was so gentle, as if he were repairing fine china.

"I should have listened to you," Autumn was finally able to manage, her voice trembling.

"Yeah, you should have. Someone else will inspect the ship from now on." There was a long pause as Frank finished with Autumn's back. "They sure knew what they wanted," he remarked. Autumn couldn't even manage a smile.

"I'm sorry Frank."

"I'm not the one who almost got raped," Frank replied, making small knots to hold the back of Autumn's shirt together. "I hope you have a spare uniform on the *Blue Jay*."

"I'm sorry for whatever I did, the kiss, anything I did to make you distance yourself from me," Autumn persisted. Frank just sighed. He gently made her face him.

"You don't have to apologize," he said as he began to clean the cut on Autumn's shoulder. "I distanced myself from you because I love you." Autumn's shock was beginning to wear off as confusion took over. "If Dale ever found out about that, he would kill your mother, then you." Autumn shook her head. Even out here, Dale was messing with her, always there.

She felt Frank's hand brush against her exposed breast as he tied her shirt into a knot at the front. She felt her face turn bright red with embarrassment. Everything had happened because she had been too stubborn to take concerns seriously. What he must have thought of her right now. To her relief, he chuckled. "You look like a tomato," he joked.

Autumn felt herself beginning to relax. He had that effect on her. She was able to manage a slight chuckle. "Thank you, Frank," Autumn replied. She meant it as a joke and as a sincere remark. Then she thought of something. "Did you pilot this thing here on your own?"

"No. Thankfully, it has a computer that can sail it without a human onboard. You want to sail her back?" Frank asked. Autumn smiled.

"Certainly." She took a seat behind the controls and soon lifted the sub off the back of the *Arrowhead*. "How did you know about the *Arrowhead's* flaw?"

Frank just shrugged his shoulders, "I didn't. I was bluffing."

"There must have been something behind your bluff. The way you stood your ground like you were actually going to shoot," Autumn said.

"Every ship has its flaws. Nothing's perfect. I had been watching the way the *Arrowhead* sailed and noted that she favoured her port side a little. I figured that somewhere along the main port, supports were a weak spot." Frank explained.

"Amazing," Autumn said. The *Blue Jay* was now in view, its markings pulsing as they approached.

"Looks like she's happy to see you," Frank remarked.

Autumn smiled. "You mean the crew is."

"No, I mean the ship. I don't think the lights can be controlled manually. They are all controlled by the computer," Frank explained.

Autumn was surprised. "When did you become such an expert on the *Blue Jay?*"

"I have been researching the ship ever since the mission, getting my hands on anything I could, trying to figure out how the hell we did what we did," Frank replied.

"I'm going to have to have a look at these documents when we get back home," Autumn stated.

"You mean if we get back."

Eastern Naval Command

"This all started because we lost the *Titan!*" Usaf shouted, stabbing his knife into the table. Usaf was the Leader of the Eastern half of the world. Since the loss of the *Titan,* the East had been regarded as weak and pathetic, and now the Western Leader was sending their weapon to destroy them.

"Sir, I don't see any other option. We have to surrender," one of Usaf's advisors stated.

"If we surrender, we will be weak. We are stronger and superior to the West. It's only because of this ship that we aren't in total control," another advisor stated. Usaf was getting a headache. They had been at this for hours and came up with nothing.

"I will not surrender! Rather than arguing, why don't you come up with a way to destroy this attack group?" Usaf asked, bringing up photos of the *Blue Jay, Shredder, Arrowhead,* and the West's newest aircraft, the *Dagger.* This was a good group. The *Shredder* had air attacks covered, the *Dagger* could destroy surface vessels, and the *Blue Jay* would take out the subs. It would be hard to get to the nuclear launch sub, *Arrowhead.*

"The two aircraft should be easy enough. They're big. They have the same manoeuverability problem the *Titan* had. The *Blue Jay* is the real challenge," the first advisor said. Usaf rolled his eyes. His advisors had great faith in their air force, almost too much.

"Wrong! The biggest problem will be disposing of the *Arrowhead*," the other advisor snapped.

This intrigued Usaf, "Explain."

"The *Blue Jay* has an entirely new crew. They got lucky last time, but it's unlikely the *Blue Jay* will survive another attack like the *Titan* ambush group. The problem is the warheads on the *Arrowhead*. If we blow that sub up, the blast radius will decimate any ships near it," the advisor explained.

"Then why don't we just destroy it and the *Blue Jay* at the same time?" Usaf asked.

"The escorts won't let us near her. We'd have to dispose of them first, to do something about the *Arrowhead*."

"Why don't we send an old sub in and, bang, it's all gone and done with while the other members of the strike package head home?" One advisor proposed.

"Alright, that's that. But we still have the problem of the *Blue Jay*," Usaf said.

"I have the answer," the Head of the Navy stated, and handed a file to Usaf. Usaf reviewed it as the man continued. "That is the *Poseidon*. It is the most advanced sub we have, developed for one purpose–to hunt and destroy the *Blue Jay*. It has more speed, more maneuverability and packs more of a punch than the old *Blue Jay* ever did–"

"What do you mean, *old Blue Jay*?" Usaf asked, throwing the file onto the table.

"The West rebuilt the *Blue Jay* after it returned to port. We don't have anything on the new model, but we're confident that the *Poseidon* can take what they've got."

Usaf sighed. It was very likely that the *Blue Jay* was now more vulnerable than before, with a less experienced crew and the fact that it now had to protect another sub. But it was also likely that the West had some surprises packed into her that would sink anything the East sent out. After a few minutes of silence, Usaf made his decision.

"I want a big strike package."

Past Crush Depth

Western Airborne Gunship *Shredder*

"Sir, look at this," the Radar Operator called. James walked over and frowned. The display showed a huge number of aircraft, ships, and subs heading right for them.

"Well, I guess these guys don't want peace after all. Get me the *Blue Jay*. Link the *Dagger* in as well," James ordered.

"You seeing what we're seeing?" Master Captain Gayle responded once contact was made.

"Yah, I don't like it. Why send so much?" he asked.

"We do have the *Blue Jay*," the *Dagger*'s Captain suggested.

James growled. He still hated the *Blue Jay*. He hated the look, the cannon on her back and, most of all, her Captain. Not only for the damage it had done to his aircraft, but his wife had threatened to leave him if he didn't start treating her better. Everything had been fine; women knew their place and men knew theirs until this stupid ship and its Captain showed up.

"It's too well prepared. They know something we don't," the Master Captain continued.

"What do you suggest?" James asked.

"*Dagger* deals with the surface vessels, *Shredder* takes airborne threats, and we'll take all subs. Our orders are to protect the *Arrowhead*, so we follow her."

"Alright! Good luck, guys!" the *Dagger*'s Captain said. Then the *Dagger* rolled away from the *Shredder*.

"Time to show off to the East. Seek and destroy," James stated. He was pushed into his seat as the *Shredder* leapt forward. In no time at all, three flights of four Eastern fighters were in view.

"Lock them and kill 'em," James ordered, and in an instant, four fighters were falling to the sea. The remaining fighters broke formation, making it extremely hard for the *Shredder* to hit them; they attacked and then just left.

That's weird, James thought to himself. The *Shredder* continued toward the flights of fighters, but they kept avoiding the big aircraft. James looked around confused. How could they just let them pass? Letting the *Shredder* into your battle group would be like sinking your own ship. Then James saw why they had retreated. They weren't needed. The sight of their replacement sent a chill down his spine. It was huge, bigger than the *Shredder* and loaded down with weapons. James slammed his fist on the transmit button on his console.

"*Shredder* to *Blue Jay*. They have a gunship! A freaking gunship!" James reported and then looked at his First Officer, "Break right and engage. Don't let that thing get to the—" Bullets raked across the side of the *Shredder*. The *Shredder* banked right and swung around to face the assailant, but it had disappeared.

"*Blue Jay* to *Shredder*, how much of a threat?" Master Captain Autumn asked.

"Bad. It can sink the *Arrowhead*," James replied.

"We're too deep. Retreat and protect the *Dagger*. She was never designed for dog-fighting," the Master Captain ordered.

"We're on our way," James said, "Helm retreat to the *Dagger*." The *Shredder*'s left wing dipped, and it pulled around.

"Sir! We may be too late!" the Radar Operator called. James rushed to his side. The display showed a 3D model of the *Dagger* with the enemy gunship coming up behind it. Another minute and it would be within firing range. James cursed under his breath.

When did they get a gunship? he asked himself as the *Shredder* banked to avoid fighter attacks. He peered at the forward camera display, which could see farther than the human eye. The enemy was right behind the *Dagger,* which was now performing "S" turns to try and avoid a missile lock. It didn't work. The enemy's guns flashed, and the right-hand horizontal stabilizer of the *Dagger* was sheared off. James cringed at the sight. That could very well be a fatal hit.

"*Dagger* to all ships. We're hit, bad. Leaking hydraulics. Multiple system failures. Still under attack," the *Dagger* reported over the radio.

"*Shredder* get in there," the Master Captain ordered.

"We're almost there," James replied, as the two aircraft came into view. "Weapons! Make them pay."

The Helmsman lined the *Shredder* up perfectly, but the enemy's nose swung upward, and it came spinning back at them, guns blazing. The *Shredder* was forced into a climb as bullets raked her belly.

"Sir, left belly stabilizer isn't responding," the First Officer reported.

"Re-engage," James ordered, ignoring the minor problem, hoping it held for now. This guy was good; he had a plan and it was going in his favour. The enemy ship kept pushing the *Shredder* higher and higher, cutting her off every time its nose lowered. They were now at 40,000 feet. It seemed an odd tactic. If anything, you would try to force your opponent to the ground. Up here, the *Shredder* had ample room to manoeuvre and avoid a missile.

James looked back to observe the enemy. It was a tough competition. The enemy had power and endurance; the *Shredder* had speed and manoeuverability.

James understood his opponent's plan and wasn't sure if they would be able to get out of this one. The *Shredder* was meant for low-level attack, with a much lower cruising altitude. If they were forced much higher, her wings wouldn't supply enough lift to keep her up, and she'd fall. As if to prove his suspicion, the computer called a warning.

"Warning. Descend immediately. Service Ceiling Exceeded." The *Shredder's* nose dipped, but once again the enemy gunship cut them up, causing the Helmsman to pull the nose back up. The stall warning blared across the bridge as the *Shredder's* wings began to shake, the ship just on the edge of a stall and still trying to climb away. Meanwhile, the enemy seemed to be able to fly perfectly fine at this height.

"Get the nose down!" James yelled, but it was too late. The air was too thin and the wing was at too high an angle of attack. The left wing stalled before the right, sending the *Shredder* into a spin. Then just as they were about to recover, the Eastern gunship delivered its final blow. Its cannons raked the *Shredder* from tail to nose. The clear bubble canopy practically shattered, then the controls jammed downward, and the *Shredder* slipped into a death spiral.

Eastern Attack Submarine *Poseidon*

"Lost contact with the gunship, sir. The last report stated they had the *Shredder* in a death trap."

Bin sighed. He hoped the gunship was all right. It was a major asset in this mission. With it gone, they were vulnerable to airborne threats. However, if they destroyed or severely crippled the two Western aircraft, it would severely limit their effectiveness.

"Let's cripple the *Arrowhead*," Bin ordered.

"Sir, our orders were to go after the *Blue Jay*," the *Poseidon's* XO said.

"Trust me, if we go after the *Arrowhead*, the *Blue Jay* will come to us."

In minutes, they had a firing solution on the *Arrowhead*, but the *Blue Jay* was nowhere to be found. Then an explosion shook the *Poseidon*. The ship slid away from the *Arrowhead* as if someone had kicked her.

"New contact. Diving fast. It's the *Blue Jay*," the Sonar Operator called.

"Sir, reports of flooding in the crew quarters and torpedo room two," the XO reported. Bin shook his head in disbelief. Not even a few seconds into their battle, and they were already leaking.

"Engage and destroy," Bin ordered, and the *Poseidon* began a turn towards the *Blue Jay*. "Remember, don't let her go straight. The *Blue Jay* doesn't like corners." The two subs continued circling each other, but neither was able to fire a shot.

"Torpedo just dropped!" the Sonar Operator called. Bin cursed under his breath. *The gunship was supposed to deal with the Shredder!* he thought to himself.

"Dive, Dive, Dive," he commanded. He knew the torpedo wouldn't be able to get them if they got deeper, or at least he hoped the information he had was correct. The bow of the *Poseidon* fell, and the ship gained depth rapidly.

"New torpedo from the *Blue Jay*." Bin slammed his fist on his armrest. He had done exactly as they wanted, gotten spooked by the surface torpedo and left themselves open for an attack from the *Blue Jay*. He heard a detonation as the first torpedo exploded.

"Dive lower!" Bin ordered. He hoped the increased pressure would cause the *Blue Jay's* second torpedo to explode prematurely.

"Sir, the ship can't go much deeper," the XO warned.

"Go deeper! That's an order!" Bin yelled. The XO nodded and relayed the order. The *Poseidon* groaned as she was pushed past her crush depth. The enemy torpedo exploded off their port side, pushing the ship even deeper, causing the frame to groan even louder. Bolts flew from their holes, flying at the crew like bullets from a gun.

"Emergency blow!" Bin called. The Helmsman didn't wait for the order from the XO; the ship lurched upwards and began to lose depth, the frame still groaning from the extreme stress. When they levelled off, the *Blue Jay* was heading straight for them.

"We have a firing solution," the Weapons Chief called.

"Fire," Bin ordered. The sound of torpedoes leaving the *Poseidon's* forward tubes filled the bridge.

"*Blue Jay's* turning...still turning...T minus 10 seconds to detonation...they're still turning...they're heading right for us!" the Sonar Operator called. Bin suddenly realized what the *Blue Jay's* crew was doing.

"Kill the torpedo!" he hollered. The crew gave him a confused look. "They're going to hit us with it!" He had read the reports. He wasn't sure if it was even possible to do what the *Blue Jay* did to one of the *Titan's* escorts, but he wasn't going to test the enemy.

"Torpedo detonated...they're still coming!"

"Sound collision alarm, surface," Bin ordered.

"Surface, surface, surface," the XO relayed. The *Poseidon* once again shot towards the surface, but it was too late. The *Blue Jay* hit her in the stern, sending the ship into a spin. The Helmsman recovered, but Bin could tell they were in trouble. He could hear the electric engines straining to move the ship.

"Damage report," he commanded.

"The *Blue Jay* hit us, there's flooding in all rear quarters and in the battery compartment," the XO reported. Bin's heart practically stopped. The *Poseidon* had two batteries, one in the stern and one in the bow, so the loss of one wasn't significant, but if seawater was in the battery compartment, it could cause an explosion that could sink the *Poseidon*. The *Blue Jay* had hit the *Poseidon* in her Achilles heel.

"Seal all watertight doors and surface, now!" Bin ordered frantically. The engines revved and strained as the ballast system groaned as it attempted to release water from the bleeding ship. However, it wasn't enough. The rear battery exploded, sending the *Poseidon* into a violent spin, throwing Bin to the deck. Alarms blared. The lights flickered, then went out altogether, and the smell of smoke filled the bridge. Bin could feel the *Poseidon* dying. Its frame cried out in pain as it twisted and bent. The depth gauge displayed a depth far deeper than the ship could take. Bin was thrown into a support beam as the *Poseidon* slammed into the sea floor.

Past Crush Depth

Western Attack Submarine *Blue Jay*

Autumn shook her head in disgust. The Captain of the *Arrowhead* had been complaining about his ship being damaged in the fight. Looking at it, however, Autumn knew the man didn't know the definition. From what she could tell, the only damage consisted of a few dents and scratches. Meanwhile, the rest of the group had taken a fair beating.

Autumn was impressed with the Helmsman; he had managed to breach the *Poseidon's* hull while causing minimal damage to the *Blue Jay*. However, he couldn't do anything about the other damage. The once new and shiny *Blue Jay* was now dented, bent and scraped, her vertical rudder yet again damaged and there was a small gash in her side that extended above the waterline. They had taken multiple near misses from the enemy subs, particularly the East's newest sub, the *Poseidon*. They also had flooding in both cargo bays, in one of the crew quarters, and the ship was leaking in the galley and a torpedo room. Autumn estimated that she had lost almost a tenth of her crew in the battle to save that ungrateful rapist's ship.

"Get the rescue crews ready on both ships," Autumn ordered as she heard the *Shredder* and the *Dagger* fly overhead. The *Shredder* had taken the brunt of the aerial attack. It had bullet holes all across its fuselage limiting its operating range to below 11,000 feet as the aircraft was no longer able to pressurize itself. It had also lost its primary firing system, crewmen, and damage to its left wingtip. Additionally, the clear bubble canopy was shattered.

However, of all the remaining aircraft and ships in the so-called "peace group", the *Dagger* had sustained the most damage. It lost one of its horizontal stabilizers and was leaking hydraulic fluid and fuel. Its flanks and wings were peppered with bullet holes and its landing gear were jammed in the down position. After the *Shredder* defeated the Eastern gunship the *Dagger* had flown high to try and avoid further damage, but it was too much. They radioed that they wouldn't be making it home. The Captain on board stated that it would be better to ditch the aircraft while they still had control. Autumn agreed. So the *Shredder* had been sent to nurse the struggling aircraft down. Now they were almost here.

The *Dagger* was far worse than had been reported. One of the engines was on fire and so was the only remaining vertical stabilizer. It also had pieces of metal hanging off of it, flapping in the wind. One piece broke off and flew into the burning engine causing an explosion that nearly flipped the *Dagger* onto her back, but she stayed flying. The *Shredder* broke its escort formation as the limping ship blaster approached the water. It wasn't an ideal day for ditching. There were waves, big enough to cause problems, and they did. Just as the *Dagger* looked like it was going to make a perfect landing, its right wing grabbed a wave, sending the aircraft into a cartwheel across the water. The ship ripped itself apart and exploded. Autumn felt her gut wrench. She thought of her cousin onboard the *Dagger*. No one could have survived that crash; even if he could have, he worked in the engine room, which was either burned or was trapped under the water as the sea claimed the dead aircraft. Autumn held back tears as she spoke.

"Order all crew back to their posts. We still have a mission to complete." Autumn was shocked by how cold her voice was. It was as if someone else had spoken. The crew rushed to get the *Blue Jay* ready to sail. Autumn didn't wait; she slid down the ladder and walked to her quarters. She reached for the bottle of whiskey but then remembered what Frank had said.

"Every time I visit, you have a drink..." Autumn shook her head and sat down on her bed. Soon a knock came at the door. Autumn righted herself and then spoke with a trembling voice. "Enter."

Frank walked in slowly.

"You alright?" he asked.

Autumn nodded her head. "Fine. Just don't like losing an entire crew."

"No one does," Frank said and sat down beside her. "Look at it this way. Three ships survived." Autumn smiled slightly. Frank always seemed to have a positive outlook on things. She couldn't remember if she had ever comforted him; it was always the other way around.

"How do you do it?" Autumn asked. Frank looked at her, seemingly confused by the question. "I mean, how can you not have a breakdown now and again?"

"To tell you the truth, I do break down. The news showing the radar data from the *Shredder* and stuff like that, it's too much," Frank responded.

"What about onboard the *Blue Jay*?" Autumn asked.

"Every second reminds me of that mission. There are times where I lock myself in the cargo bay and just cry."

Autumn was taken aback. He was being so open. A year or so ago, he never would have admitted that. "Why don't you come find me?"

"You have enough on your plate already. The last thing you need is to worry about me," Frank stated.

"That's BS. You comfort me all the time. I could return the favour," Autumn said, harsher than she meant to.

"Autumn, I don't think you would be able to," Frank said, getting up and walking to the bottle of whiskey on the counter.

"Why not? I have those moments as well. Flashbacks of the mission, the *Titan*, Sounder's death, everything," Autumn snapped.

"I don't break down because of that," Frank stated and handed her a glass of whiskey. He hadn't poured himself one. "You looked like you wanted it."

"Then what the heck makes you break down? I'm your friend, Frank. I want to help," Autumn pressed.

"You, losing you," Frank stated plainly. The glass of whiskey fell from Autumn's hand and smashed onto the floor, shattering into hundreds of pieces. She knew he loved her, but she didn't know how much. She also knew she loved him. She'd known ever since he rescued her from the *Arrowhead*.

"Now you see why I don't want to worry you with this," Frank said and turned to leave. Autumn grabbed his arm.

"You can talk to me about anything, Frank," Autumn whispered. She stood up and kissed him. It was a deep, lustful kiss.

"I love you," she purred softly when she broke the kiss.

"What about Dale?" Frank asked.

"Screw Dale. I'd rather die than let you walk away," Autumn replied. "You promise you'll come to me if you need help?"

Frank smiled and grabbed her. "On my love for you."

Autumn's smiled broadened. She was finally able to say what she wanted, and Dale couldn't do anything about it. There was no way that he could learn of this so far from the West and so deep in the sea.

"Master Captain Autumn?" a voice called over the intercom in her cabin. Frank chuckled softly.

Of all the goddamn times, Autumn thought to herself as she pressed the mic button. "What?"

"Call for you from the *Arrowhead*," the voice responded.

"What do they want now?" Autumn asked.

"Apparently our baffles are worsening the damage to their controls," the voice said. Autumn shook her head.

"These guys don't know the first thing about damage," Autumn grumbled to Frank. Frank just laughed. "Tell them I'll be right up."

"Certainly, Ma'am," the voice said, followed by the distinctive click of the intercom being turned off.

"I better go," Autumn said. "We aren't done here. Dinner here, tonight. Just me and you. Hope you don't miss it."

"Wouldn't for the world."

Western Defence Command

"What do we know?" Dale asked as he walked in. He had been at the hospital when he got the call telling him the East wanted to talk. On top of that, Autumn's mother had just died, removing all leverage he had on Autumn.

"Report from the *Blue Jay*," a lieutenant responded, and hastily handed Dale the report. Dale read it and frowned. All ships but the *Arrowhead* had extensive damage. His frowned deepened as he read the part of the report regarding the *Dagger*. Under status in bold red letters was printed:

Destroyed No Survivors.

That was the newest aircraft the West had and now it was lost. This only amplified his concerns for Autumn. If the *Dagger* went down and the *Shredder* had been severely damaged it meant the East had something very powerful. Dale sat down heavily. He didn't truly care much about the *Dagger's* crew, or the other men lost. They were numbers to him. The crew could be replaced; the loss of the ship was another thing. The only crew that concerned him was one Captain, Autumn. He should never have sent her on this mission. The screen in front of him lit up, displaying the leader of the East, Usaf.

"You ready to surrender?" Dale asked, still reading the report, he saw something that boosted his confidence.

"Hardly. I warn you for the last time to call off your ships or I have no choice but to destroy them," Usaf stated.

"I will not recall them. Surrender or face the consequences," Dale spat.

"You have your report. You lost an entire ship and the others are damaged; they will not survive another attack." Usaf said. Then the screen displayed the *Shredder* and another large aircraft battling. It wasn't a pretty sight. The *Shredder* was losing, its wings shot up, and the entire aircraft scraped and burned. Then *Shredder* fell into a spin only to recover and have the Eastern aircraft nearly blow the clear canopy off the bridge as the *Shredder* fell into a death spiral. The video ended and the Eastern Leader reappeared. "Call them off or this will be the fate of your entire attack group!"

"You're starting to sound desperate. I remember a conversation like this a while ago. Back when the *Titan* was still afloat," Dale mocked.

"You are signing your own death certificate."

"Perhaps, but at least I won't die defeated," Dale continued, "Surrender or I worsen the damage."

"Very well. Say goodbye to your precious *Blue Jay.*"

"I'm not too worried. Seeing as the *Blue Jay* has already destroyed your most advanced sub," Dale said, waving his report at the Eastern man. He signalled the operator to cut the call and the screen went black.

Western Attack Submarine *Blue Jay*

"Ma'am, looks like there's another wave coming," the Sonar Operator called. Autumn brought up the sonar display on her wrap-around panel. He was right. Four ships were waiting for them just off the Eastern shore, and one sub that was far to the south.

"Alright, order the *Arrowhead* to push deeper and tell the *Shredder* to pursue and destroy," Autumn ordered. The crew rushed to get this done and soon the bow was lowering.

"Ma'am! *Arrowhead's* ignoring its orders! It's ascending!"

Damn it, Autumn thought to herself. She didn't think that even a Captain as idiotic as the one on the *Arrowhead* would risk the ship just to spite her. No, he had his orders. She had long thought this mission was more than a peace attempt. No, the *Arrowhead* was going to do something ordered by Dale. She cursed, then turned to Frank.

"Circle back and get that sub," she instructed.

"And the *Arrowhead?*" Frank asked.

"They have their orders and we have ours," Autumn replied. Frank nodded and relayed the instruction. Soon the *Blue Jay* was pulling a tight turn and heading for the enemy sub. Then, they were right alongside it. Autumn thought it odd that the crew lets a threat get so close; she had a bad feeling about this.

"Sonar, do they see us?"

"Negative Ma'am," came the reply.

"All silent," Autumn ordered. This order made the *Blue Jay* almost impossible to detect but also made it vulnerable. It involved shutting down the props and drifting along with its momentum; the crew would be ordered not to speak unless necessary.

"Light it up," Autumn commanded. The huge lights on the side of the *Blue Jay* snapped on, and what Autumn saw made her cringe. Limping along next to the *Blue Jay* was a beaten sub with a large hole in her stern. Even without the name written on the bow, the enemy sub was unmistakably the *Poseidon*.

God must hate us, was the first thing that came to Autumn's mind.

Western Nuclear Launch Submarine *Arrowhead*

"We're at firing depth, sir," the XO reported. Lardo nodded. He wished he could have seen the look on that Master Captain's face as he ascended away from her ship, completely ignoring her orders. It felt good to put her in her place. He breathed a sigh of relief. Now the *Arrowhead* would make its mark on history.

"Prepare to open hatches," he ordered. The only flaw with the *Arrowhead's* missile launch system was that the ship had to surface to open the launch doors or, risk flooding. For that reason, surfacing was the last step in the procedure.

"All clear Captain," came the report

Lardo smiled, *Show Time*, "Surface and prepare to fire." He turned to the XO. The two men moved to the firing control. Lardo removed the firing key from around his neck and placed it into the firing control.

"On three?" the XO asked.

"On three," Lardo responded, "One...two...three." With that, Lardo and the XO turned their keys. The display lit up and one by one the firing lights for each missile silo began to illuminate. The missiles would climb steep and fast till they reached their cruising altitude where they would fly toward their targets and then dive on them. Lardo wanted the launch to finish quickly, so he could dive back down to safety. Suddenly, the *Arrowhead* lurched sideways and the stern was pulled underwater as a tremendous explosion echoed throughout the ship. The firing control display lit up with the words.

ERROR 124; UNSTABLE LAUNCH PLATFORM, MISSILE 8 LAUNCH ABORTED.

Lardo cursed his luck and then rushed to the center of the bridge.

"Seal the launch hatches. Dive and recover," he ordered. Although the dive order was irrelevant, the *Arrowhead* was already gaining depth, quickly. "Damage report!"

"Flooding in all rear compartments. Engines are inoperable and the controls are unresponsive. All ballast tanks have been breached," the XO reported.

"What hit us?" Lardo asked, though he knew the answer. The *Arrowhead* had been on the surface of hostile water. Two torpedoes from nowhere could have easily done this kind of damage. He closed his eyes and sighed. His orders stated that if the ship was compromised, it should be destroyed to remove all evidence of the attack. However, he wasn't about to commit suicide.

"Emergency blow," he ordered.

"It's no use sir. The ship is dead," the XO prompted.

"No. The *Blue Jay* made it back, so will we," Lardo insisted. He turned to address his crew only to be tackled to the ground. Two crew members held him down as the XO relieved him of his firing key.

"I'm sorry Captain, but orders are orders," the XO stated. He quickly overrode the computer and set the last remaining nuke to launch with the hatch closed. The detonation would destroy the *Arrowhead*. But the *Blue Jay* and the *Shredder* could fly home safely.

"You'll kill use all!" Lardo protested.

"We all die if we return anyway," the XO responded and turned the keys. Seconds later fire filled the mid-section of the ship and she was blown to pieces.

Past Crush Depth

Eastern Attack Submarine *Poseidon*

"Sir, sub off the port side! It's the *Blue Jay*," the Sonar Operator reported. Bin slammed his fist into his armrest. Of all the luck! The *Blue Jay* had found them when they were vulnerable. The *Blue Jay* had caused extensive damage to the *Poseidon*, destroying one of her two diesel engines, the stern battery, crippling the one spinning prop and killing a large number of the crew. Further, the frame had been severely compromised. The only thing that had allowed them to survive was quickly closing the watertight doors in all undamaged compartments of the ship. Even then, they were just within operational weight limits. Bin had hoped to make port before the *Blue Jay* reached them, but that had not worked out.

"Prepare to engage," he ordered.

"Sir, you can't possibly think we can beat them, do you?" the XO asked.

"They beat the *Titan* while they were severely damaged. We can beat them," Bin said calmly.

"Sir! *Arrowhead* is launching missiles," the Sonar Operator reported.

"Damn," Bin muttered. "Break from the *Blue Jay* and destroy the *Arrowhead*."

The *Poseidon* pulled away from the *Blue Jay*, its frame producing large groans of protest from the stress. They swung around and headed right for the *Arrowhead*, which was a sitting duck on the surface.

"We have a firing solution," Weapons reported.

"Fire tubes one and two," Bin ordered. Employing the only still functioning launch tubes of the four on board. The torpedoes found their mark; the crew was rewarded with a satisfying explosion and the sound of bulkheads tearing. Bin smiled. Even crippled, the *Poseidon* was able to inflict severe damage. However, Bin wasn't prepared for what came next. The *Arrowhead* exploded. A huge underwater nuclear blast. The shock wave hit the *Poseidon,* and it buckled. Its stern tore clean off, and the control tower crumpled as the sub ripped apart. It hit the sea floor in hundreds of pieces.

* * *

When Bin woke up, he was in a dark room. He could hear water gushing and could feel it pooling around his body. Feeling around in the dark, he deduced that he was in what was left of the bridge. He crawled to the emergency exit hatch, grabbed a respirator and pulled the lever that blew the hatch open. Water rushed in, pushing him against the wall. Once the pressure equalized, he crawled out and was met with a horrible sight. The *Poseidon* had not just been destroyed; it had been pulverized. The control tower lay at least 10 feet from the rest of the sub. He then saw something else. The *Blue Jay*, lying on her side, markings glowing dimly in the murky water, still in one piece. Bin couldn't imagine how strong the frame had to be for the ship to survive that explosion.

No matter, he thought, it was on the floor; none of the crew could have possibly survived that impact. Then the prop began to spin. The ship was alive; the crew still running her, living inside. Bin exploded frustration. *What does it take to kill this thing!?* he asked himself angrily. He felt there would be no upside to living. He would be publicly executed for his failures if he returned to the surface or killed by the *Blue Jay's* crew if captured. He removed his respirator, releasing his last breath, he let the water fill his lungs.

Western Attack Submarine *Blue Jay*

Autumn grunted in pain as she rolled onto her back. The *Arrowhead*'s blast had hit the *Blue Jay* hard, driving her onto the sea floor. Autumn had been thrown from her seat but never lost consciousness this time. The lights flashed and flickered as she tried to sit up, but a fire of pain ripped across her chest, preventing her.

Great, she thought. She must have broken some ribs. Her legs moved, but when she tried to put some pressure on the right leg it felt like a knife stabbed her.

"Broken," she muttered. She managed to crawl towards the helm. She was disoriented; it felt like the ship was laying on its side, but she figured it to be just a head injury. A shower of sparks erupted from the ceiling as she reaches the Helmsman. She gently shook him trying to wake him up, she quickly stopped and choked back sobs. The young man had so much potential. The way he handled the *Blue Jay* was incredible. But an inch and a half wide hole in his chest told Autumn he was lost forever. She looked away from the body and caught a glimpse of the orientation display. It's showed that the *Blue Jay* was in fact on its side. The blast must have been worse than Autumn had thought if it rolled the ship. She looked to the port side windows and her heart sank. They were cracked, badly. The windows held, but another near miss with a torpedo would surely break them.

Autumn swallowed hard and continued to Frank's seat. He was still strapped in, but blood covered his face. She shook him, more violently than the other man, wanting desperately for him to wake up.

"Frank, wake up," she whispered. All around her she could hear men grumbling and grunting. It sounded like the majority of the bridge crew was alive. Autumn's mind flashed back to the bridge of the *Blue Jay* just after the impact during the last mission. Bodies everywhere, men dying, all because of her.

"Goddamn it Frank, wake up," she sobbed, punching him in the chest. Frank coughed and grunted.

"Autumn?" he asked weakly.

"I'm here," she responded, grasping his hand. She could hear people beginning to rise but she didn't care. She hadn't realized how much she feared losing Frank till right then and there.

"Why did you punch me?" Frank asked, running his figures over the contours of Autumn's knuckles.

"I thought you were dead," she said. "You alright?"

Frank just chuckled, "I hit my head, you?"

"Ribs and leg, nothing serious," Autumn said.

"Ma'am?" the COB asked behind them. Autumn rolled herself to a sitting position propped up against Frank's chair.

"Yes?"

"Uhm...I have the station preparing damage reports; should be ready in a few minutes. Would you like help to get to your seat?" the COB asked. Autumn shook her head.

"Come here," Autumn instructed, and the COB knelt down beside her. She used him as a crutch to get back to her seat, although sitting was a bit of a challenge. She activated the wraparound display, which to her relief worked perfectly. Reports and data began to pop up from all sections.

"We have flooding in all portside compartments, but nothing serious. They are all contained and we are still within operations weight limits. Sonar reports no submerged or surface contacts. Engineering reports flooding but engines are still in good working order..." the COB continued his report.

In the end, the *Blue Jay* could sail, but wouldn't be much good in a fight. Autumn sighed heavily, and then inhaled sharply as her ribs attack her.

"Get us sailing, will you?" Autumn ordered.

"The relief Helmsmen requests that you do it as he has never done it before," the COB replied. Autumn smiled. She limped to the controls and sat down heavily. It was interesting sitting down on the sideway chairs, but not impossible. She gripped the wheel and instantly the light snapped back to normal and the markings, visible through the cracked windows, glowed brighter. Autumn's smile broadened, the ship was alive. She carefully eased the *Blue Jay* off the bottom, with only slight groans of protest from the frame. Soon she had it steaming away.

"I trust you can take it from here?" Autumn asked the relieved Helmsmen. The young man nodded. "She's all yours."

Once Autumn made it back to her seat, now righted, she reviewed the reports. "COB where are the reports from the *Shredder*?"

"We don't know Ma'am, we can't gain radio contact. They're up there, though; looks like they're still engaging Eastern fighters."

"Order them to break and run," Autumn stated.

"Right away." The COB turned to the radio operator. The sound of tearing metal filled the bridge along with splashing and an explosion. Autumn froze, she didn't even want to guess what gave way. Whatever it was, it sounded like it would sink the *Blue Jay*. Something hit the bow, then another hit at the stern.

"Lights," Autumn ordered. The lights snapped on the illuminating wreckage of something big hitting the *Blue Jay*. The explosion hadn't been from the sub, it had been something else tearing apart. "What do you think crashed, XO?"

"Autumn," Frank called. That was the first time Frank had called her by her first name on the bridge in front of the crew; she quickly turned and practically broke down.

The lights on the *Blue Jay* illuminated large pieces of wings, engine, and frame twisting, breaking, sinking, and one very large distinctive tail with the words *Shredder Gunship* printed on it.

Poor Debra, she thought.

Western Attack Submarine *Blue Jay*

Frank handed Autumn a glass of whiskey and she graciously took it. With the *Blue Jay* steaming home they were both finally able to take time for themselves. But even though they won the battle, Autumn felt like she had lost the war. Sure, a lot more of the *Blue Jay*'s crew had survived, but she had also lost three other full crews. A burden she would always carry. On top of that, she had Dale. This thing with Frank would have to come to an end once they got into Western waters. It would break her heart, but she was sure not even Frank would put up with her relationship with Dale forever. Autumn took a large sip of her whiskey.

"Well, we survived," she said quietly.

Frank nodded. "How are you doing?" he asked.

"I'm shaken," Autumn responded.

"It's going to be okay," Frank said somewhat distantly. Autumn didn't want to go home. She wanted to say right here, out in the *Blue Jay*, under the waves. But she knew that would only create problems. Dale would come looking for her. If he thought someone stole her from him he would shoot, and the *Blue Jay* couldn't take much more damage.

"I have to tell that sweet girl that I let her husband be killed," Autumn sighed.

"There was nothing you could have done," Frank stated, taking a sip of his water.

"Wasn't there? I could have called them back sooner. Seen where this was going and split. Called everyone off and let the *Arrowhead* fend for itself. There was so much I could have done but didn't because of my own goddamn fears," Autumn shot.

"Get over yourself. There was no way you could have known anything. Besides aborting the mission would result in execution."

This hit Autumn hard. "Frank we need to keep this thing between us a secret. I don't want you killed," Autumn said.

Frank nodded. "It was worth it,"

Autumn smiled. Then the phone beeped. Autumn walked over and picked it up.

"Call from HQ Ma'am," the operator said. Autumn frowned and covered the mouthpiece.

"Don't make a sound," she told Frank. He nodded in response.

"Put 'em through," Autumn instructed the operator, and soon her aunt was on the line.

"What the heck are you doing at HQ?" Autumn asked.

"I needed to speak with my son. They told me to call you," her aunt stated. Autumn felt guilt swimming inside her again.

"There's a problem with the *Dagger;* you can't speak with him right now," Autumn managed, her tone ice cold. She didn't want to tell her aunt that her son had been killed protecting that rapist's ship.

"Well, let me know when I can. By the way, I'm so sorry about your mother," Autumn's aunt replied. Autumn almost did a double-take.

"What happened to my mother?" she asked, getting very worried.

"You haven't heard?"

"Aunty I've been at the bottom of the sea for the past few weeks," Autumn responded quickly, wanting to move this along. "What happened?"

"Autumn, sweetie, your mother passed a few days ago."

Autumn let the phone fall from her hand. *Dead? I must have heard her wrong,* but deep down Autumn knew she'd heard her aunt correctly. Frank got up from his seat and put a hand on Autumn's shoulder.

"Everything all right?" he whispered. Autumn shook her head. Frank reached over and hung up the phone. He then turned her towards him and gave her a hug, patting her hair.

"My...my...mother..." Autumn tried to explain, but she couldn't stop sobbing. Frank held her tighter.

"It's alright, let it out," he said softly. And Autumn did. She just stood there crying on Frank's shoulder, her leg starting to hurt from the pressure. Had Dale found out about them somehow? She wondered. Or was it natural? It didn't really matter anyway. She was gone. At the same time, all Dale's leverage was as well, but that did very little to comfort her. Instead, it only made her cry more because it only meant Frank was next.

Past Crush Depth

Western Attack Submarine *Blue Jay*

Autumn stood on the back of the *Blue Jay* once again, as it pulled into its home port. The *Blue Jay* looked somewhat better than it had last time it returned from a mission, but it was still battered. If Autumn turned around she would be able to see the cracked windows of the bridge. Even where she stood there were dents and huge scratches across the ship's sides where the wreckage of the *Shredder* had hit them.

Then she noticed something odd. One of the Western destroyers in port had its gun turret moving. She grabbed her radio.

"XO, there's a destroyer with a moving turret up ahead."

"We see it," Frank responded.

"Arm the cannon and put fish in the tubes. I have a bad feeling about this," Autumn ordered. She couldn't imagine port security being so sloppy as to allow Eastern men onboard that ship, but with success could have come arrogance. It was more likely, though, that Dale had staged something to give another reason to attack the East. The only question was, what was their target? The destruction of the *Blue Jay* would be an open card for Dale to level the East, but it would also destroy morale and make success all that harder. Maybe he had found out about her and Frank. Autumn felt guilt creep into her heart. If she had doomed all the remaining crew because of her own desires she would sooner kill herself than live with it. To her relief, though, the gun turret continued past the *Blue Jay* and rested pointing at the shore. Autumn followed its line of fire and saw a tent, set up to provide shade for Dale who was welcoming the *Blue Jay* and her crew home. She reached for her radio then stopped. If she let the ship fire then she could be rid of Dale, all her restrictions, everything. She would be free to live her own life. She considered the consequence. Her mother's life was no longer on the line but would she be punished for not firing? It seemed unlikely. No one else had noticed the ship. How could they expect her, a woman, to notice something the superior male sex, hadn't? She quickly made her decision. Of all the lives she'd ended, she would feel the least guilty about Dale's. If anything, he deserved all that was coming. She left the radio and waved to some people on the shore. She didn't even flinch when the destroyer fired. She looked to the shore in time to see the explosive round decimate the tent. Then she grabbed her radio.

"Fire," she ordered. In seconds, she heard two torpedoes speed away from the *Blue Jay* followed by a tremendous boom as the *Blue Jay's* cannon fired. The cannon shot hit first, blowing a hole on the water line, then the torpedoes blew the ship to pieces. Autumn forced herself not to smile, and quickly retreated to the bridge.

"Dock quickly and get all emergency crews ready to help," she commanded. She was trying to seem a bit worried but it wasn't working. She exchanged a short glance with Frank before walking back towards the loading bay door.

Once the *Blue Jay* docked, Autumn disembarked and rushed to the burning tent along with the *Blue Jay's* rescue workers. When she got there firemen were pulling bodies from the blaze. She went up to one, put on her best panicked face and asked.

"Dale?" The fireman shook his head.

"Sorry Master Captain. The shell hit right at his feet." Autumn lowered her head to hide the relief bubbling up inside her. She was finally out of his reach. He could no longer mess with her. She limped back to the ship, where Frank was just coming down the gang plank. She smiled at him.

"You didn't fire?" he asked.

"I thought it was for a ceremonial shot," Autumn lied. Frank just shook his head chuckling and gave her a hug.

"Master Captain Autumn Gayle!" someone called from behind them. Autumn turned and guilt stabbed at her once again.

"Debra," she stated softly.

"How did this time go?" the young woman asked. Autumn straighten herself and tried to minimize her injuries.

"Hell," she replied. Debra and Frank started to laugh and Autumn managed to join in. "I'm sorry Debra. This is Frank. He's the *Blue Jay's* XO."

"I know, he was on the original mission, used to command the ship before Captain Autumn took over," Debra said happily, shaking Franks hand, "I'm a bit of a fan of the *Blue Jay* and her crew."

"Happy to meet you," Frank said, still smiling.

"So where's the *Shredder,* I can't wait to see the data from the mission?" Debra asked. Autumn and Frank exchanged a look. Autumn took a seat on a nearby bench and motioned for Debra to join her.

"How bad was the damage?" Debra asked, her face showing her growing concern.

"Debra...we lost the *Shredder.* No one survived the crash," Autumn stated.

"What, no! How?" Debra stammered evidently trying not to cry.

"I don't know. We got hit hard and we were just regaining control when it went down. I'm so sorry." With that Debra began to cry, she leaned on Autumn and Autumn did her best to comfort her.

176 Catwalk Drive

Autumn grabbed the two plates of food and limped to the table. Her leg was broken but she had a walking cast so she could still move about. She heard a knock at the door and her heart leapt. She moved towards the door as fast as possible, which wasn't fast, only her cast had other plans. She tripped and fell to the floor. She rolled herself onto her back and heard the door open. Frank quickly helped her to her feet.

"How many times must I tell you to just say 'come in'?" he asked. Autumn smiled and gave him a kiss.

"Dinner's waiting," she said simply. Frank helped her to her seat. She didn't need it, but it was nice that he did it anyway.

"So how did it look?" Frank asked after they were seated.

"Better than last time, but still damaged," Autumn responded.

"I still can't believe that she's being repaired."

"It's the symbol of the Western Navy, they want that thing floating as long as possible," Autumn stated, "I met the new Leader."

"How was that?" Frank inquired, after swallowing a forkful of noodles.

"It was good. He was a supporter of mine when we went out the second time," Autumn explained.

"A man supporting females in the Armed Forces?" Frank asked.

"Yah, surprised me as well. Apparently the Eastern Leader was killed by the *Arrowhead's* attack and the East and West are going to try for peace," Autumn finished, rolling her eyes. Frank just laughed.

"Give it a year and the *Blue Jay* will be attacking them again. This meal is really good by the way."

"Thanks. Twenty-five bucks at the store down the street," Autumn said, laughing as well. He knew as well as she did that her cooking was less than mediocre.

"So what happens now?" Frank asked.

"I will continue commanding the *Blue Jay* until I am unable to—"

"So when you're dead," Frank interrupted. Autumn smiled.

"Yes. As for you...I could get you your own sub," Autumn said dropping her voice at the end of her statement. She didn't really want him on another sub. It would mean separation from each other for months at a time and the continuous possibility that he wouldn't come back.

"I don't want my own sub," Frank replied.

"No Frank, you deserve it," Autumn insisted.

"Autumn, I don't want to serve on any other sub," Frank stated firmly, "Or serve under anyone else's command." Autumn felt her smile broaden. She moved out of her chair, wrapped her arms around his neck and kissed him.

"I hoped you'd say that."

Acknowledgments

I would like to acknowledge the contributions of Sharyn Heagle, who provided moral and technical support along with knowledge to which I would not otherwise have had access. Without her, this book would not have been possible. Thank you, my mother, Betty Gloutney and to Melody Tomka for her assistance in editing this manuscript. Finally, thanks to my family and friends who stood behind me and put up with the process of my writing this manuscript. Thanks to you all.

Born in Nova Scotia, Patrick Gloutney always held an interest in storytelling: Putting pen to paper at a relatively young age. After moving to Ottawa, and interest in writing grew. He was awarded 2nd place in the National Capital Youth Writing Competition in 2013. He continues to explore various approaches to writing alongside pursuing his other passion, aviation. An active member of the flying community, he has been repeatedly recognized for his dedication, enthusiasm, and professionalism in his craft.